ROCK
MY
WORLD

Rock My World

Fiction: Romance Thriller

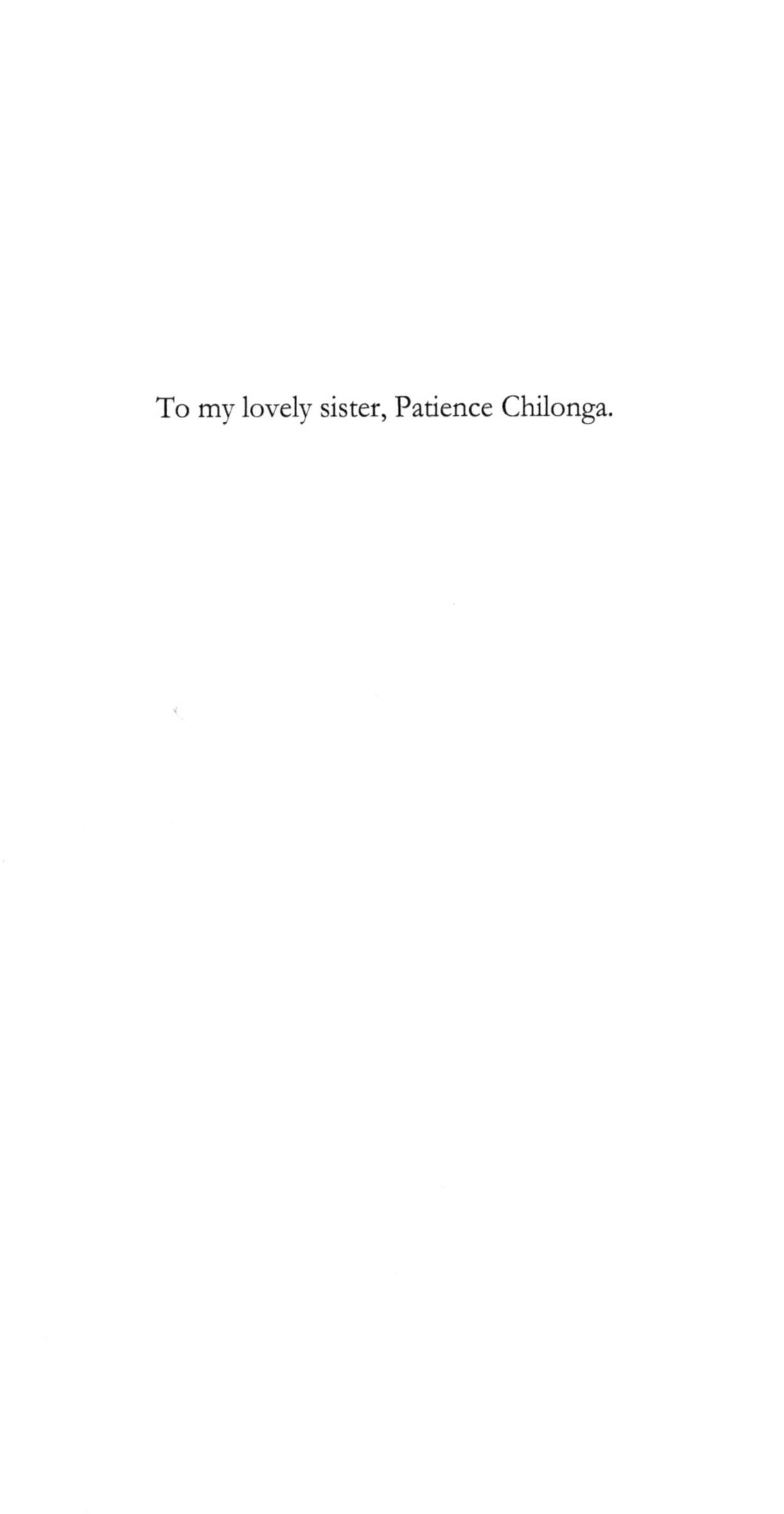

To my lovely sister, Patience Chilonga.

Table of Contents

Chapter One

"You can not go. It won't be safe out there for you. You have never been to another city before. And alone?" But Janet proved adamant, she had made up her mind and whilst she parked some of her best dresses, she knew that not even her mother could talk her against her decision. "There are many local musicians here. Why don't you go to their concerts instead. As your mother, I forbid you from taking such a drastic and stupid step."

"I can easily go to any local musician's concert but I can't miss this opportunity to see Mathew. It is his first time here in Canada and I bet it will be his last. Don't worry mom, I will come back after the concert is over."

"I can't talk you out of your decision now, can I?"

"No. . . I didn't go online and buy the first ticket for nothing. I have been holding on to this ticket for three weeks now. Did you think that I wasn't serious when I told you that I wanted to see Mathew perform?"

"Your father will kill me when he learns that I let you go."

"I will call him immediately I arrive in Timmins," Janet said and closed her small suitcase of ten different change of clothes. She carried the suitcase and walked out of her bedroom. She was determined to go, her mother had obviously realized that and just stared at her go.

Mathew was an American rock musician, he had made his debut barely a year ago but his popularity had grown both in America and in Canada. People cued up for his concerts, his tickets would be auctioned for and Janet was lucky that she was one of the first people to have learned of Mathew's scheduled performance in Canada where he would start performing firstly in Timmins and would later go on to Vancouver, Quebec, Ottawa, and Toronto during the course of his tour.

Janet was an instant fan of Mathew ever since his career began. She planned on going to Timmins for the one show she managed to have a ticket for. Mathew was scheduled to have three shows in Timmins. Two immediately when he came into Canada and the last after he toured the country. After attending the first show, Janet planned on being outside or backstage for the other remaining shows just to get a glimpse of the famous Mathew. So she planned on staying in Timmins for one week, the scheduled time Mathew was to be in the country.

"Do you at least have enough money for the trip?" her mother inquired immediately Janet had walked out of the house.

"Don't worry about me mom, I will be fine," she responded and walked away from the house. Her mother waved at her but she walked fast from the yard, determined to quickly get out of there.

When she reached town, she boarded the cheapest means of transport possible, she boarded a train to Timmins. Her mother had been right, it was her first time out of Saute Ste Marie and she did have the feeling of being alone when she walked out of the train and stood with her small suitcase in the subway. She was finally in Timmins. She walked out of the subway and when she was outside the train station, she reached for her pocket and released a small paper which had an address written on it, the only address she knew in Timmins, the venue to Mathew's concert. It was scheduled to happen later that day and so it was in the vicinity of that venue that she wanted to be in.

But whilst she waited for a cab to the concert alongside the road from the subway, she couldn't help it but stare at her small suitcase. It was an obstacle and she couldn't take it to the concert. She also knew that the hotels in the area around the concert would be expensive but she needed a place to stay to wait the week. Deciding to look for accommodation in the residencies from the subway, she turned left and walked in the direction of the residences. She stared at the environment she was in, it wasn't that different from Saute Ste Marie. This made her wonder why Mathew had chosen to make Timmins the first and last city for his tour of the country. It was cold in Timmins and she was only grateful that she had her sweater on. Wind kept blowing past her brown hair, and she could feel the cool wisp of air on her face.

After she had walked a considerable distance, she looked to her left where she saw rows of buses with people getting off some of them and boarding others. It was a busy day and she knew why. Many people looked busy, and many were her age. But she needed a local, someone who seemed not interested with the activities of that day, an elderly member of the community, someone who knew the city too well. So whilst holding her sweater in place, Janet walked on and when she saw a man walking lazily with a woman, possibly his wife, she approached them for directions. She needed a hotel to stay in and she asked them just that.

Later that evening, she was at Mathew's concert. She was close to the entrance and it would be just a matter of minutes before she could be allowed inside the venue. Having had managed to find herself a humble room at one of the local hotels, she was only thankful to the couple who had taken their time to walk her to the location of hotels in the city. Now that she was at the venue, she struggled to stay in line as it was both noisy outside as it was chaotic on the line. Security in front was tight and the guards there were very strict about tickets. When she approached them, she was sure to have her ticket in hand. She stood on her heels, smiled at the guards and handed them her ticket which they inspected, put a stamp on and gave back to her. She entered the concert to a hall crowded with people. Knowing that she would miss most of the fun which would happen in front if she remained in the back. So while people chatted along and others stood silently, waiting for the arrival of the much anticipated rock musician, she struggled her way to the front until she was by the demarcation between the performance and the crowd.

She closed her eyes and tears began to roll out of her eyes when she heard the crowd erupt, she knew that Mathew had finally arrived. She opened her eyes to the first ever performance of Mathew she would watch away from television. It was a surreal moment and as Mathew played his guitar, Janet was certain that moment was worth her trip from Saute Ste Marie.

At the height of the show when Mathew sang his hit lead on the album he had announced would be out later that year, she felt as though he was singing the song to her. Suddenly everybody and everything was blotted out and she could only see Mathew. It was at that point that she knew that she was in love with the musician. Mathew put on a wonderful show and at the end of the song when everybody erupted in applause, she felt as though she had been shaken up from a good dream. She had been staring at Mathew and now that she had seen him up close with eyes like she had never seen anyone before, the song was over. She stared around and joined in the applause but unlike the wild crowd, she only clapped her hands very slowly as if she had been caught doing something wrong.

Even when she felt her phone vibrate in her hand, she dared not pay attention to it despite knowing fully well that it was her parents calling her. She had promised to call home as soon as she had reached Timmins. Janet reasoned that must have been her father calling her probably to reprimand her on the decision she had made but she just couldn't take her eyes off the dashing young man as he bowed to the crowd after a wonderful performance. Mathew's wavy hair and a bad-boy aura to him had an intoxicating effect on her and as she clapped along, she decided that it must have been love she felt for Mathew. She had never dared to go away from her house before. But standing there amongst all those other Mathew fans, she had taken a bold step of leaving her home city for another despite her having little money on her. Even though she knew that she would die with that love, she wanted to live in that moment.

"Having a great time miss?-- My name is Josh!" one guy spoke loudly to her and extended his hand to her but she only stared briefly at him, irritated that he could disturb the magical moment she was experiencing there. She stared away from him, disregarded him and continued to stare forward but what she saw in front sank her heart. Mathew lost consciousness and fell on the upper pavement from the stage during his walk to his band after he had saluted the crowd.

The crowd immediately fell silent, a couple of girls cusp their hands on their mouths probably in fear and concern for Mathew. But Janet couldn't just stand there, she was filled with concern and deep worry and even without realizing that she had dropped her phone, she dared to cross the boundary which had been set up by guards and security of the concert. She ran towards the stage and the police who had been trying to contain the crowd at the other side began to run towards her. Mathew, on the stage, was surrounded by security and his band that it was difficult seeing him. One police officer was almost upon Janet. Realizing that she couldn't get to Mathew on time or fast enough before she was caught, she got off her high heels which were slowing her down and she tightly held her purse whilst her other hand held her skirt in place. By doing that she ran faster and managed to dodge the heavy hands of the policeman who kept begging her to calm down and control herself. She got on the stage and climbed a stair, she stared up in time to see Mathew being carried along through the back door on the stage. He looked unconscious and exhausted. She ran after him and thankfully there was no one on stage to stop her. She went through the door that Mathew had been taken through and kept praying and hoping that nothing bad could happen to Mathew. Outside, she saw Mathew slowly regain consciousness as he held the rear of the black car he was being pushed to enter into. He slowly looked to her before he entered into the car. He looked exhausted and sick but Janet was only glad that Mathew would be okay.

She stood at the back of the concert and watched Mathew's procession go before she realized she also had to go. It was very late at night and she knew that it wouldn't be safe for her out there. She looked at herself, she was barefooted and she also realized that she had lost her phone. She reasoned that going inside to look for it would be futile. When she stared at her red purse which perfectly matched the red dress she wore, she was glad that she had enough money on her to pay for a cab.

Once she was safely in the room of the hotel and on her bed, she couldn't help it but worry about Mathew, it was his first concert there in Canada and yet he looked so exhausted and so weary. She knew the incident of Mathew's collapse on stage would be on the news and she felt sorry that could be the last time she could see Mathew again because she was sure that after that incident, his manager would immediately arrange for transportation back to America for treatment and would also cancel all his scheduled concerts in Canada. But she had booked a room for a week and the hotel strictly mentioned that it didn't entertain refunds, so she would have to stay back even despite the reason for her coming there would have gone back home.

Before she could sleep, she turned on a radio (the only pass-time in the room she had booked) and after a couple of music, they did have news on Mathew, but nothing that she did not already know. She reached for the radio and turned it off and for the lights too and tried to sleep off the worry that she had for Mathew.

Early the next morning, she got up, yawned into the mirror, and took a quick bath. She put her makeup on and after breakfast which was offered as part of the hotel's room service, she went out of her room to the hotel's reception and found a bored receptionist there. It was early in the morning and Janet wondered why the receptionist would be bored that early. She, however, didn't care to find out. She just proceeded to talk to her about what she had come there to do.

"Good morning," Janet said, startling the receptionist who now focused her eyes on Janet after appearing as though she had been in deep thought and her mind had been somewhere distant.

"Yes?"

"May I use your phone? I lost mine at the concert yesterday."

"You mean at Mathew's concert?"

"Yes, why?"

"I was also there," the receptionist said, smiled and handed the phone by her desk to Janet "I am a huge fan of Mathew's"

"Me too," Janet said, glad that she had found someone who shared her interests and as she dialed her father's number she couldn't help it but notice the broad smile of the receptionist after she had heard Janet tell her that.

"My name is Rosemary," the receptionist said and extended her hand to greet Janet, she noticed it in time before she could punch in the last two digits, she held it firmly and smiled.

"My name is Janet, I am from Saute Ste Marie."

"I have an aunt there. I love it that side, I visit there frequently, that is if I am not required to work here. I am sure we will be friends."

"We already are," Janet said and slowly released Rosemary's hand, she continued to stare at her and Rosemary stared back, also smiling "If you are no longer required to work here, why don't you make time to visit my room, it is room 5 on the fifth floor and we may catch up on news about Mathew."

"You bet I will," Rosemary said whilst smiling at Janet and staring at her as if she had said the best thing she had heard that morning. Janet too, was glad that she would have someone to talk to during her week's stay at the hotel.

"Now that we are friends bring that phone to me," Rosemary said. Confused, Janet stared at her. She was only one digit away from talking to her father and now this? She reluctantly gave the phone back to Rosemary..

"Why?"

"Because I want you to use my phone instead. I insist. I am guessing you want to talk to your boyfriend back home and I know you need privacy," Rosemary said, grabbed the hotel's phone from Janet's hand and put it back on the desk, she gave Janet her phone instead, "Take your time."

"I just want to talk to my parents"

"Still-- return it to me as soon as you are finished."

Janet quickly punched the numbers on Rosemary's phone and brought the phone to her ear and she heard the line connect to her father's phone in Saute Ste Marie. Before she went up the stairs, she looked at Rosemary who stared at her, smilingly and expectantly with an interest too noticeable to ignore. Janet mouthed a 'thank you' and Rosemary, still smiling mouthed a 'welcome' and Janet walked away from her and went up the stairs.

When she had just reached the second floor her father picked up the phone. Janet was reluctant to speak, she did not know what to say after she had left home without saying anything to him. Knowing that he was furious at her, she decided to calm him on phone other than confront him at home.

"It's I, Janet"

"It is Janet, honey. Come and talk to her because I don't know what to say to her," Janet heard her father say.

"Janet--Janet are you alright?" her mother, after a few seconds, talked desperately on the phone.

"I am alright. Why this deep concern for me. I told you that I would be fine here and I am," Janet said and continued climbing the stairs, she was now on the third floor. "Is father mad at me?"

"No darling, he is relieved that you are safe," Janet's mother said. "Not relieved. Tell her that she is grounded for a month once she gets here and she better forget about that job of hers. That meager money is making her do stupid things!" Janet heard her father tell her mother. "Don't worry about him. We all love you and are glad that you are okay," Janet's mother continued on the phone. Her father interrupted again, "Don't tell her that." But her mother talked on, "We heard that you were probably arrested at Mathew's concert, and we are on our way to Timmins right now. Your father even got to absent himself from work. You know he never does that--"

"Who told you that I was arrested?"

"A boy called using your phone. He said he wasn't sure about your arrest but he was certain that you were being chased after by the police when you ran on stage at the concert right after Mathew lost consciousness--Why would you do that?"

"What consciousness. What police?" Janet tried desperately to lie but she heard her father speak to her mother, "Give me the phone!" and after some seconds her father spoke to her on the phone, "No more concerts for you missy. We are coming to Timmins and you better be ready for the trip back home," he said and cut the call.

Janet knew that she was in serious trouble now. She couldn't talk her father out of what he had decided and whoever that boy was, who had called her parents using her phone had put her into so much trouble. Holding limply Rosemary's phone, she climbed the stairs to the fourth floor and then to the fifth floor where her room was located. Her visit had been cut short and she knew better than to not be ready when her father came over. She still knew that her parents didn't have the address of the hotel she was staying in but she decided not to tell them, at least not then when her father was very upset with her. The trip to Timmins had taken her two hours by train and she knew that it would take her father only an hour in his car, she therefore decided to call after thirty or forty-five minutes and only hoped that by that time he would have been calm.

She opened her door, walked into her room and went straight for her small suitcase, she did not have much to pack and she was done in less than ten minutes and sat on her bed and waited for thirty minutes so that she could call her father.

She looked at the radio, then over to the mirror and on the mirror stand was her red, purple, and blue purses and her kit of mark-up. She had forgotten to pack those. Going over and rushly grabbing the items, she went back to her suitcase and put them there also. It was now fifty minutes since she had last talked to her father. Even though she didn't have the guts to call him back, she knew she had to. However, she found herself staring at the phone in her hand. And then it rang and it was her phone number which registered and she knew that the call was from the boy who had called her parents with distressing news about her. How she hated that boy. Not only would she lose her job because of him but she would also be home bound for a month and would not go to any concerts ever besides the fact that she loved music so much.

Without hesitation she answered the phone call and placed the phone tightly to her ear. She was angry at him.

"Who gave you the right to talk to my parents!?"

"Uh. . . my name is Josh, remember the guy at the concert?"

"I don't care what your name is. I just asked you a question!"

"Who did you want me to call after I picked up the phone at the concert yesterday?"

"Thank you Mr Josh for being so mindful and informing my parents that I was arrested."

"I know right, they were so worried and I am only glad that you weren't arrested. The show was intense yesternight-- and by the way, you have a lovely family. I didn't know that you were from Saute Ste Marie. I had thought that you were from around here."

"Are you done?"

"What do you mean?"

"I want my phone back."

"Just give me the address of where you are staying and I will--"

"So you think that I am stupid like the random girls you meet at concerts. Never. I will never give you my address."

"Uh, I think we got off on a rough start. Shall we start over. . . My name is Josh--"

"Are all boys here stupid like you are. You still don't get it do you? I don't care about what your name is and I won't give you my address. I just want my phone back."

"Fine, then come and get it at Crystal hotel. I work there and I will leave it by the entrance gates. Just tell the gateman that you require the phone left by Jo-- since you don't want to hear my name. I won't tell you and we shall see how you will get the phone from him, miss Janet," the boy said and cut the phone call.

"Wait," Janet managed to speak but the call had already been cut. She had heard his first name but she surmised that wouldn't be enough to make the gateman at Crystal hotel give her the phone. So, she called her phone number back but the phone was switched off.

"Idiot," Janet managed to say and climbed off her bed.

Realizing that her parents were now in Timmins, she summoned up courage to call her father. It was in the company of her parents that she wanted to go to Crystal hotel and get her phone back.

"Dad," Janet said into the phone.

"Yes dear?" Janet's father responded, surprisingly calm and composed that Janet wondered what was wrong with him.

"You must be in Timmins by now. I live downtown in Moreal hotel, room number 5 on the fifth floor, when you reach the hotel be sure to consult the receptionist-- Rosemary. She's a friend. She will be more than glad to show you the direction to my room. This is her phone I am using right now."

"There is no need to worry. Your other friend-- Josh, the one who had the trouble of picking up your phone after one of your childish-- I mean, he has promised to bring you home himself. He is a charming boy if I may add. Nobody goes through the trouble of helping out strangers anymore. He has convinced us to stay back home and your mother and I can not wait to meet him."

"Sure, dad," Janet said and cut the call.

"What a scumbag, I am sure he is up to something," she silently said to herself before she opened her room door. She was dumbfounded at how Josh would assure her parents that he would personally bring her back home and why they could be convinced to stay back and not see through his tactics. But she had, she could not be fooled that easily. Josh wanted to take advantage of her but she wouldn't allow him to. Her parents could be comfortable with a stranger providing escort for their one and only child but she wasn't as trusting as they were and she would get to the bottom of his act. She had told Josh that she was not gullible and stupid and she had meant it. Knowing what boys his age wanted from random girls they met at concerts, she was sure she wasn't going to be one of those easy targets. She was a lady and she knew how to handle boys like him.

She walked down the corridor, down the stairs and soon the reception was visible to her. She saw Rosemary speaking to one man and Janet reasoned that must have been a customer, she climbed down and waited by the stairs for Rosemary to finish talking to the man before she could proceed to go to her desk. And in a couple of minutes she did finish speaking to the man, gave him room keys and smiled at him go. Janet then approached the desk.

"Thank you for the phone," Janet said and handed the phone to Rosemary.

"You are welcome," Rosemary said and put the phone behind her desk.

"What time does your shift end?" Janet asked.

"At 6 p.m-- I planned on visiting your room immediately I got off work."

"Will you escort me to Crystal hotel when you get off work?"

"Sure. Are you going to see someone special at Crystal?"

"You would say that," Janet responded, Rosemary giggled. "Because I plan on giving him special red marks on his cheeks," Janet added and Rosemary laughed.

"Did you two have a fight?"

"I don't even know the stupid boy."

"Tell me more," Rosemary was on tip toe, and her eyes sparkled with interest. Janet leaned closer to her desk and said in a whisper.

"When I was at the concert, right when Mathew fainted this boy tried to approach me--"

"Who does that?"

"Exactly-- so I ignored him and ran on stage to check on Mathew--"

"You don't mean you were that brave and courageous girl in the red dress?"

"Yes I am."

"I am lost for words! Did you see Mathew up close?"

"Oh yes! But he wasn't looking so good. I only hope he is okay."

"Me too."

"But the boy picked up my phone and called my parents and told them I was arrested. He had got me in so much trouble that my parents thought of coming over here to get me. They should have been here right now if not for that boy again."

"What did he do?"

"He told them to stay back and that he would personally take me to them."

"How sweet," Rosemary had now put both her

hands under her chin and was attentive at what Janet was saying. She had a dreamy expression that Janet didn't expect her to have.

"You don't understand. He is trying to take advantage of me using my phone. He asked for my address after I told him I wanted my phone back but after I refused he offered his address instead and seeing that my parents would escort me to the hotel to get my phone back-- I don't know how he did it but he managed to make them stay back so that he and me could be alone at a hotel. I have read through him and I know what he is trying to do."

"And I won't let him. You should make that two slaps because I am also going to give him a piece of me," Rosemary said.

Later that day, after 6 p.m., right after Rosemary had got off her shift, both girls stood in front of the five star Crystal hotel after they had been dropped off by a cab. They both stared at the hotel, amazed by its beauty and enormity.

"I know. It is marvelous here. I don't tire from looking at it each time I pass by. I live down this road so I look at the hotel each day I go to Moreal. I just wish that one day, I will work here. That is my dream, how marvelous would that be?" Rosemary said whilst she continued to stare at the hotel.

"Yes it is lovely and I can only wonder how many girls Josh has lured inside that hotel. I bet he is only a gardener there, but he says 'I work there' as if he holds an important job in the hotel."

"I didn't know you despised him that much."

"I despise anyone who puts me against my father. You can't understand, I work so hard so that he must be proud of me and now this random boy comes from nowhere-- forget it. Lets just go."

Rosemary followed along and Janet led the way as if she knew the place. The sun was setting and it would be dark soon. In front of them was a big black gate and wonderfully adorned. As she approached, she had a feeling that she had stepped upon the yard of a very rich man that she was hesitant at first to approach the gate and knock or press a button (she wasn't sure how she would make entrance into such a place) but she was glad that as soon as she arrived at the gate, the gate opened by itself and out from it emerged a black van with tinted glasses that made her wonder what secrets the car held. The car looked creepy. Why would anyone, unless he had something to hide, want his car glasses tinted?

Taking advantage of the opened gate, she walked faster towards it and urged Rosemary to hurry up. But Rosemary seemed to have been lost in the sight of the hotel. It was clear to Janet that Rosemary had never got a chance to come that close to the hotel. Rosemary did, however, hurry up and she was soon walking side by side with Janet and both girls were soon past the car. Janet turned around and saw the tinted, all black car, enter the main way and speed in the direction

Rosemary had hinted her house was located in.

Coming towards the gate, Janet could hear heavy voices argue whilst the gate was slowly closing by itself. She and Rosemary had to hurry to get inside before they were locked outside and had to knock or ring something for the gatemen, whom Janet reasoned were the ones arguing, could open the gate for her.

"Is she here yet?" Janet heard the familiar voice say. She instantly recognized the voice as Josh's, she had been bothered by him at the concert and she had talked to him on phone that she could not mistake his voice. That soft, calm, yet irritating voice could only be Josh's. After she realized that, she relaxed, she wouldn't have to wait, ask for him or explain herself to the gatemen.

"Did you hear that?" Janet asked Rosemary. Rosemary shook her head and continued to stare in bewilderment at the hotel inside. Janet had to pull her hand for Rosemary to notice her.

"I didn't hear anything," Rosemary said, asserting what she had meant when she had shaken her head.

"keep it down and listen. I think Josh is inside that guard room."

"Really?"

"Yes-- that is where we need to go." And the girls walked towards the guard house which was just a few meters from the gate they had entered from. They walked towards it whilst they quietly paid attention to what was being talked about in there. Rosemary after learning that Josh was inside, she stopped staring at the hotel in the front right and instead stared curiously at the guard house, obviously interested or curious about Josh and as the two girls approached the guard house, the male voices grew louder that it was almost creepy and scary. Janet was approaching a group of men and she didn't know what their intentions were especially when they were friends with someone as cunning and unscrupulous as Josh. But she reassured herself. She was with someone and if the men tried anything funny, she would scream or call the police. She stretched her hand out to Rosemary, but Rosemary stared at her blankly. 'Phone' Janet mouthed. Rosemary understood and handed her phone to Janet who quickly punched in the police's emergency number, intending to press on the call button the moment she noticed anything fishy or phony at the guard house they were now very close to.

"How many times do I have to tell you that no girl matching that description was here. No, she has not yet come. What is it you want with her anyway?" one of the men in the house said.

"I want to give her something and I am surprised she has chosen to leave it and go home."

"What is it?" another man said.

"Her phone-- I told Mr Jod here. I am surprised he hasn't told you yet."

"Why should I tell him? It is not like you were expecting someone important," the man whom Josh had called by the name Jod interrupted.

"You don't understand. She is important to me, and I knew that the moment I saw her. Her eyes, her laughter and oh, her charm, I like this girl. I really do--Just send her to my office if at all she arrives, please even if I am busy, I will make time. Even if it's tomorrow, I will be available."

"Don't you have that meeting with the board tomorrow?"

"I said that I will be available. Just don't let me miss the opportunity of seeing her."

"You are in luck. Here I am scumbag," Janet said after pushing open the slightly opened door. Two men, as old as her father, sat down behind a small table and Josh stood opposite them, his back to the door and when she entered into the room, all three of them stared at her, they all looked surprised. Rosemary stood closely behind her and Janet closely held Rosemary's phone and her finger rested on the call button. Anything funny from the astonished three men inside that guard room, and she would press on the call button.

"How romantic," one of the men opposite Josh finally said and both men laughed. Josh, however still looked astonished but tried to approach her.

"Not another step!" Janet said, held up Rosemary's phone and showed it to Josh "Or I will call the police."

"Good pick Josh, son. Good pick," another man said and both laughed even louder.

"You didn't tell me that Josh is so handsome,"

Rosemary whispered behind Janet.

"Not now Rosemary," Janet whispered back to Rosemary. She then looked ahead to Josh, "Give me my phone back. Nobody is going to your office today," she said.

Josh in the frozen position put both his hands in his trouser pockets. He looked radiant in that black suit that he had worn. And surprisingly his cordial and relaxed demeanor returned. He was no longer surprised and his emerging smile proved to Janet that although Josh had been startled by her entrance, he was nonetheless glad that she had made it to the hotel.

"Your phone is in my office. There is no need to be afraid, be more like your friend and relax." Janet stared back and found that Rosemary was smiling at Josh. She was startled at her behavior and shook her.

"What is wrong with you?" Janet asked between closed teeth.

"I am sorry Janet-- Mr Josh, you heard her. We know your plans. Just give us back our phone!" Rosemary said, clearly overdid it but Janet was glad that Rosemary had returned to what they had come there to do.

"What plans?" Josh asked, shrugged and looked behind at the two men who continued to laugh.

"Police!" Janet said and was about to press the call button when Josh realized that she was serious.

"Okay," Josh said, reached inside his pockets and released Janet's phone. "I just wanted to talk to you that's all."

Rosemary walked from behind Janet to Josh and grabbed the phone from his hand. And before Janet could brink, she saw Rosemary slap Josh very hard across the right cheek, that the sound rang in Janet's ear for a few seconds too long. Josh had slightly closed his eyes and opened them in an expression of pain.

"Never you think that we can not defend ourselves. Such a good looking boy trying to take advantage of innocent girls like us," Rosemary said and immediately as if the room couldn't get any louder, the two men laughed loudly than before. Josh looked pitiable as he stood in the middle of the room seemingly not knowing what to do. He was embarrassed and the smile which had been on his face was wiped out. He now looked funny where he stood and as Rosemary approached Janet, Janet had to pull her quickly towards the door because she didn't want to imagine what Josh would do to them if he got out of the shock he was in.

The two girls walked quickly out of the guard room with Janet pulling Rosemary as they walked forward. They did not look back and Janet was glad that someone in the guard house had the mercy to let them out of the hotel because as soon as they came to the black gate did it open and walking fast out, the two girls were soon by the main road, waiting for a cab.

"You over did it," Janet said as a cab pulled over.

"I know-- but did you see the look on his face?" Rosemary responded and they both laughed. She got into the cab and said, "I will see you tomorrow. I will arrive early than I usually do and I am coming straight to your room. We have a lot to talk about, don't you agree?" Rosemary said and held her cheek in mock pain. She giggled and Janet smiled.

"Yes Rosemary. Have a safe journey home."

"Sleep well," Rosemary said and the cab was gone. And in a few minutes another pulled off and Janet got into that one, told the driver that she wanted to go to Moreal and relaxed. She was happy that she finally had her phone and would never have to see or talk to Josh again.

Chapter Two

When she was at the motel, she grabbed a quick shower and had a quick dinner and slept . Before she slept off immediately it was 9 p.m, she learned that Mathew had canceled his second show in Timmins and that it was not certain what his plans were after he had collapsed on stage. But the radio caster hinted at the possibility that Mathew would cancel all his concerts in Canada and return home. The news came as a sad development to Janet because it confirmed that Mathew was still sick. Knowing that there was nothing she could do for him, she slept with a heart weighed down by worry and concern but glad that she wouldn't have to put up with Josh anymore.

She thought of calling her parents to inform then that Josh would no longer be taking her home as they had hoped but decided that she would do so the next morning. Early in the morning. By then she hoped to have figured out a good lie to convince her parents that it had been Josh who had refused to take her there because they had sounded as though they were expecting him.

Early in the morning whilst she was in her sleep, she heard a knock on her door and another. At the fifth knock she woke up. Yawned and stretched herself up and rushed to the door. Rosemary had promised her that she would be in the motel early and Janet therefore knew that it was her knocking on the door.

She reached for the handle of the door, half asleep, and pulled the door open but it couldn't bulge. She realized that she hadn't unlocked the door yet and so she turned the keys and when it was unlocked she pulled the door open once again and who she saw standing in the doorway, smiling and holding a huge bouquet of pink roses startled her and immediately had her heart beating fast inside her chest.

"You!"

"I am sorry for yesterday. Here except my flowers to you as a sign of my apology for my behavior yesterday," he said and handed the flowers to Janet.

Janet didn't know what to do. Was she to take them or reject them. It didn't feel right to reject the flowers. They smelled so good and it didn't feel right to accept them either. That would give Josh, the boy in her doorway hope that she might also be interested in him. She therefore chose the only option plausible to her at that moment, she stepped back a few steps inside her room, her heart still beating fast, and slammed the door in the face of Josh and went back to her bed to sleep and to pretend there was no one at the door.

Josh knocked once and then twice. He called her name and called it once more but Janet pretended not to hear, she pulled her blanket over her head and after a few minutes, Josh quit trying and Janet surmised he was waiting at the door in doubt of what he was to do next.

She tried to sleep but she had woken up and after several minutes of hearing nothing from the man on the door, she pulled her blankets off her head and went to the bathroom, she brushed her teeth, combed her hair and wondered how Josh had gotten hold of her exact address at Moreal especially given then that she had been glad that she had gotten rid of Josh and that he couldn't bother her anymore. She thought to her parents, besides Rosemary, they were the only ones who knew of her address at Moreal but she brushed off the thought, she didn't want to think so lowly of her parents. They couldn't have given her address to Josh. She was therefore sure that Josh had followed her to her motel.

Then she heard a familiar knock. She looked at the door in consideration from her dressing mirror but she had already made a resolve to drive Josh away.

"Go away!" Janet said.

"It is me, Rosemary"

Janet got up and went to her door. She opened it and saw Rosemary standing in the doorway. She was staring at the flowers in her hand, smilingly. She walked in even without being invited in as she sniffed on the flowers quiet heavily. The flower odor, soon filled the room and Janet couldn't help it but admire the flowers and notice what a beautiful collection they were.

"I have been here all my life and no one thought of bringing me such a gift. Whoever sent you this must be in love with you," Rosemary said.

"Or he is after something," Janet responded sharply.

"No. . . don't tell me these are from--"

Janet nodded and went to sit down on her bed. Rosemary soon joined her after she put the flowers in front of the dressing mirror.

"He was just here. I am surprised you did not see him when you were coming here."

"No. . . I could have known him, after all I did slap him yesterday. I just passed by a man exquisitely dressed and smelling good if I may add-- No, that was him?"

Janet nodded once more and fell on her bed.

"You may get the flowers if you like them that much. I don't need them."

"Really?"

"Consider them a gift from me to you."

"Thank you. I know just where to put them. Tell me everything that happened," Rosemary said. Janet got up and sat properly and recounted what had happened that morning to Rosemary. But Rosemary still insisted that Josh's behavior was charming and nothing short of love would have made him apologize for something he did not do wrong.

"But he had asked me to his office," Janet protested.

"Still we were the ones who were rude to him. We slapped him, remember?"

"You slapped him."

"I think the boy likes you. He is handsome. He works in a good place. What more can you ask for?"

"Love. And unfortunately I feel nothing for him," Janet truthfully said. Rosemary laughed.

"What?"

"You just met him yesterday. Get to know him and I am sure you are going to develop feelings for him."

"You don't understand."

"What don't I understand?"

"I am in love with someone else."

"I see."

Later that day, the two girls were still chatting, Janet had to remind herself that Rosemary was working at Moreal but the condition of the place made it easy for them to chat about. Hardly any customers came by. From Janet's room, Rosemary went to work and Janet followed her along. The two talked about everything. She told Rosemary about Saute Ste Marie and Rosemary told her everything about Timmins. When it was nearing lunch, they agreed to dine together and they ordered a sumptuous meal. They sat on the table close to the entrance of the motel, a few inches from the reception desk and ate whilst they spoke.

"Is it always like this here?"

"Meaning?"

"Business. Customers," Janet said and took another bite.

"Today was a busy day. And the other was when Mathew arrived in Timmins. So if you are worried about the slowness of business wait till the regular days. Business is so slow that I had made boredom my friend. That is before you," Rosemary said and chuckled, she took her drink and stared at Janet. "Honestly, I am going to miss you when you are gone."

"Me too. My house is always open for you in Saute Ste Marie."

"Please promise me you will also visit me here. I live alone and it gets lonely there."

"Why wait for that long. What about I visit you today. After 6 p.m.?"

"Really?"

"Yes friend," Janet said, smiled and continued to slowly chew her food. Rosemary looked delighted and Janet was sure that if it hadn't been for the table the two were sited opposite each other, she would have reached for her and hugged her for the great news she had told her.

Two customers walked into the motel. Rosemary stood up and followed them. She immediately went from Janet's view. Janet had to turn around to watch her go to the reception desk. Janet looked past Rosemary and the two customers to her desk where she saw the rose flower bouquet she had put on the reception desk for display. Rosemary walked behind her desk. She attended to the customers and when they went towards the stairs, she stared ahead at Janet and lowered her head on the flowers. She sniffed on them heavily and smiled at Janet. Janet smiled back and looked away from Rosemary and after a few seconds, she heard her come towards her. She went behind her chair and grabbed it.

"I am excited for today," Rosemary said.

"Me too," Janet responded.

"Guess what I thought of when I sniffed those flowers and starred at you?"

"I am not good at guess games. If such are the games in your house, I am afraid I may change my mind about sleeping over there tonight."

"Don't joke like that. I am sure you will love it at my house."

"I am sure I will-- What did you want to tell me. That you thought about me and Josh?"

"Close but no. I thought about what you told me in your room this morning."

"I am listening."

"I wanted to ask. No, no, I wanted you to tell me about that boy you said you are in love with," Rosemary said. Janet blushed, she smiled, she thought about his wavy hair, about how good he looked whilst on stage and a deep worry came over her when she remembered how he had fainted on stage after his last heartfelt performance. A song which he had sang to her. She stared blankly at Rosemary and realized that she would only dream of Mathew.

"Someone is definitely in love-- Will you tel me or are you going to continue staring at my plate like that all day?"

"There's no future in my love for the boy."

"Why do you say that?"

"Because the boy I was talking about is Mathew."

"What!-- Do you know how many girls have a crush on him. I am also in love with him, I mean who couldn't be. If you ask me, you should probably give Josh a chance-- he is handsome, charming and adorable. Learn to distinguish between fantasy and reality. Josh is your reality and Mathew a fantasy. Every girl's fantasy."

"You are probably right. I was thinking the same thing also."

Rosemary finished eating her food before Janet finished hers, Janet ate slowly as she considered what Rosemary said to her. She repeated in her head, 'she is probably right' and when she finished eating she looked over at Rosemary, smiled and slowly stood up.

"Where are you going?"

"I had forgotten to call my parents. I want to talk to them and I will be down after I do that."

"Don't forget to tell them about me."

"I already did," Janet said. Rosemary smiled and

watched Janet go.

Janet was disappointed and walked hurriedly to her room, she didn't want Rosemary to realize how disappointed she was. The one time that she thought she had found true love had turned out that it was only a fantasy and she could as well forget about it. Rosemary had claimed that she, like many girls, loved Mathew too. She hurried past the fourth floor and ran down her corridor to her room as she realized that she was exactly what she claimed she was not to Josh--stupid. And considering what her father had told her, she might as well be childish. It was time to grow up and live in reality. She had rejected a lot of guys too many before Josh and she wasn't getting any younger.

Once she was inside her room, she slowly sat down and pushed her back towards the back of the door and the door closed as she pushed backwards and finally it was closed. She continued to sit there with her back against the door and slowly located her father's phone number in her phone. She knew that what she was about to do, she would not reverse. But if Josh made her father happy, she was willing to settle down with him. Her father never liked anyone, she therefore surmised that Josh had some good qualities to impress her father as he had done and she couldn't argue with her father's choice for her.

"Dad. . . Josh has a meeting today. So he can not bring me home."

"You may come alone. He can visit anytime. Tell

him he is more than welcome to do so."

"No, I would rather wait for him. I will inform you when he is not busy and ready to accompany me to Saute Ste Marie."

"Okay dear, pass my greetings to the young man."

"I will Sir. Pass my greetings to mother. . . And Dad?"

"Yes dear?"

"I love you."

"I love you too," Janet's father said and hung up the phone.

Janet put the phone down and stared at her bed and then at the mirror and over at the wall from the door leading to the bathroom. She awaited a loveless marriage. But she knew that her father knew what was best for her.

She sat in that position for a few minutes and then for a few hours and tears started rolling out of her eyes. She quickly wiped them out as she became dumbfounded at what was making her cry. She then heard a knock. She stood up and for the first time hoped that it was Josh at the door but when she opened the door, it was Rosemary standing in the doorway, smiling as usual.

"Is it time," Janet asked, surprised at the amount of time she had spent sitting there behind the door.

"Yes it is girl's night out!" Rosemary said jubilantly "Are you ready?" Rosemary said and walked into the room.

"Of course," Janet said and wiped the few tears which were under her eye lids, careful not to ruin her make up.

Rosemary had taken great pains to make sure everything was perfect for Janet. She had bought good food for supper and had arranged for someone to clean up and decorate her place before the both of them went there. When they were there they chatted until late into the night and only woke up with the help of three alarms in the morning. Janet could have sworn that was the best night she ever had indoors, the music was great, the food was delicious, the surrounding was perfect but Janet had been troubled about how she could summon courage and the bravery to go to Josh. She had assured her father that she would go home with him and the fact that Rosemary hadn't realized how troubled she had been all night was amazing or was it because she had put up a good act before her for her to notice.

Early the next morning, the two girls came together to Moreal. Janet and Rosemary walked into Moreal together after both had greeted the receptionist at the desk whom Rosemary was supposed to take over from, both girls proceeded up the stairs, and down the corridor to Janet's room, giggling and laughing about the previous night. In the distance both girls saw another bouquet of flowers. It was big about two times the size of the previous one. And the corridor leaked of a heavy odor of sweet perfumed flowers and it was intense as they got closer, intense for anyone to ignore it. Both Janet and Rosemary were surprised and quietly but quickly approached the flowers.

Janet was the first to touch the flowers, she passed her hand over the pink and assorted roses. What lovely flowers they were and over to the back of the flowers she saw a hurriedly written note. She knew it must have been from Josh, she opened it and read quietly whilst Rosemary was all over the flowers, examining them with a heartfelt admiration.

On the note was how heaven was short of angels because one was on earth and it was signed Josh. Janet only reasoned that Josh was referring to her but she was not moved. How many boys had told her that before that it had lost its magic since the first time she had heard it and now a grown man like Josh resorted to such phrases which the high school boys had decided to neglect. It was at that moment that she realized that Josh hadn't dated much. She might as well be his first and considering what she had heard him tell the guards at the guard house at the hotel, she was almost certain that it was his first time chasing after girls and at that she was impressed at his effort. The flowers were extraordinary despite the note. She folded the note and gave it to Rosemary for her to read.

"I can't believe he hasn't given up on me after that day at the hotel and also after yester-morning."

"Wow! I am touched," Rosemary said as she continued to read and re-read the note. Obviously she too, hadn't received a lot of love messages.

"Keep the note and I will keep the flowers," Janet said. Rosemary tried to protest but Janet said, "I insist" and when Janet saw that there was no way that Rosemary would get the card with Josh's name written on it, she opened the door, carried the flowers inside and looked about her room for a pen before she realized that she didn't have any. "Do you have a pen?"

"Yes, sure. Why?"

"May I borrow it?" and Rosemary searched through her hand bag and released her pen which she handed over to Janet.

Janet grabbed the note from her and went over to her dressing mirror where she placed it down. She canceled Josh's name from the card and stared in the direction of Rosemary who stood between the door and Janet's mirror, confused and starring at Janet obviously wondering what Janet wanted to do.

"You never told me about your love life. Or you dodged it when I asked you repeatedly over at your house."

"I must be late. We will catch up on that later."

"You see what I mean?"

"What?"

"Do you have a boyfriend?"

"No why would I?"

"That is a pretty stupid answer."

"I have to go."

"You are not going anywhere until you answer my

question."

"Also mine is an impossible love."

"I get it you must be in love with Mathew too," Janet said and quickly wrote Mathew's name on top of the crossed out name of Josh. She was about to hand it to Rosemary before she heard Rosemary speak again.

"No not him. You can't understand."

"Our friendship has grown stronger, hasn't it? You are starting to sound just like me," Janet said. Rosemary chuckled and walked towards the door very slowly but Janet noticed her go.

"Not so fast," Janet said.

"You will hate me when I tell you my truth."

"Try me."

"I am in love with my brother okay. I made an excuse and ran away from home because of that and I have been living alone for five years now."

"A great decision. Because your brother is fantasy and here--" Janet handed the note she had scribbled the name of Mathew on to Rosemary, "this is your reality." Rosemary looked at the card and smiled, she shook her head but tightly held the card in her hand.

"You are something," she said and opened the door. She stepped outside. Janet waved at her.

"Thank you for yesterday and I will be down there for lunch," Janet said and Rosemary walked away.

At lunch time, the two girls sat at the table they had sat on the previous day. They ate quietly this time with no one trying to raise a topic and when Janet was into the meal she decided she had enough. Both of them couldn't continue like this anymore. She had to clear the tension and she knew that the only way she would get that done was if Rosemary could speak freely about her problem to her and not feel embarrassed about it like what she was feeling there. She looked as though Janet had peeked on her doing something extremely wrong. Extremely evil. And Janet wanted to assure her that was not the case.

"It must be admiration you feel for your brother."

"I am grown up, I know what I feel."

"I understand. But you can talk freely to me about it," Janet said and another minute of silence erupt between the two ladies. "So, does he come to visit you?"

"Yes he visits but infrequently."

"Why is that?"

"Because I am always unavailable and I did not tell him where I worked from. We were close when we were little. If he knew where I worked from, he would never miss a day to come here."

"But you do know that your love is far fetched. I mean, it is more impossible than is mine and Mathew's."

"Don't you think I already knew that. Why do you think I ran away from home?"

"Does your brother know about your. . . feelings?"

"Not even in my nightmare would I tell him."

"I think we are friends for a reason. It was fate

which bound us together, we have the same destinies. . . loveless. . . alone--"

"Josh is a great guy, I am sure you will fall for him eventually."

"And when that happens, I will ask him if he has a brother,a cousin or something. I will not let you continue to live alone. You also deserve to be loved and to love again."

"That will be great," Rosemary said, smiling. "I am always open to love and maybe I may finally forget about my brother."

"So, Where does your brother work?"

"He is still in high school."

"He is younger than you?"

"Yes-- by about three years," Rosemary said.

And just when the conversation couldn't get any weirder, a few minutes before Rosemary would have to go back to her desk and resume work, the two girls heard a loud noise in their ears. It was nothing like what Janet had heard before and the sound was just outside the motel and judging from how horrible the sound and how loud it was, it was a few centimeters from the entrance of the motel.

Janet looked over at Rosemary. She too appeared surprised and she was sure that she also had an opinion which would be similar to hers. How could a person exist who was so talentless that at a beautiful musical instrument like a guitar, he would produce such horrible sounds which made music appear like one big joke.

"Do you want to check it out?" Rosemary asked as she darted her eyes to the direction the sound was coming from.

"Only if I can tell him to stop."

"We will both tell him so and if he refuses, I think I have some money on me. We will give him that. I am sure he will go away. This has never happened before, but I guess the street kids have grown inventive over the years," Rosemary said and both girls burst out of the motel laughing.

The entrance of Moreal motel attracted a wealthy crowd of people. And others stared down at them from their motel windows across the streets. However none of them looked amazed at what they saw. Janet surmised that like them, they were irritated at such a disturbance, in such a quiet and peaceful neighborhood.

Janet pushed past two people who blocked the entrance of the motel as she wanted to glimpse at the men who were singing Mathew's hit single but in the hands of them it sounded like just words, rantings and nothing rhythmical about them. She looked at the group of three musicians, one on the drums, the other on the keyboard and another with a guitar strapped across his chest and a microphone mounted on the open yard. Janet looked closer at the one with the guitar and she did recognize him. It was Josh and from the way he stared at her, he too recognized that Janet was approaching them with Rosemary closely following from behind.

"This is the height of craziness," Rosemary said.

"I know. How is it that I may make him go away. He has clearly lost it," Janet added.

Janet saw Josh go to the microphone and speak into it.

"Make way for my princess. The one I solenade today. Even though I am just a simple accountant, I can become a rock star for you. This is for you Janet!"

And before she would go any farther, the attention seemed to have shifted from Josh to her and people stared at her that she became embarrassed at the attention Josh created for her.

However, Josh in front proceeded to produce the horrible sounds from the guitar which he claimed were music. He knelt down and sang a song which was both romantic and enthralling in the hands of Mathew the rock star but which had lost its appeal in the hands of Josh. She knew she had to stop him. He was obviously the leader of the three-man band and Janet therefore knew that immediately she stopped him, she would spare the neighborhood the trouble of listening to him. She knew that immediately she stopped him, then the men on the drums and on the keyboard who were also as horrible as he was would also stop.

"Stop!"

Everybody looked at Janet. Josh remained in his kneeling posture but was quiet now, the other men he was performing with, too, became silent. Everybody waited for her to speak. Josh looked at her, expectantly.

"You have won over my heart."

"Just like that?" Josh asked but his two friends seemed happy because they proceeded to drum insanely and the other pressed runatically on the keyboard, that even though Janet had been sure that the sound couldn't get any worse, it did.

"I said stop!" Janet shouted on top of her voice.

"You heard the lady guys, don't destroy my chances now," Josh pleaded with his friends.

"I am sorry for that. . . You may go back to whatever you were doing and I promise you this will never happen again," Janet said, the crowd dispersed. Josh looked happy, relieved and his eyes sparkled with happiness. He did not look calm and composed but rather ecstatic as if his best dream had been fulfilled. He continued to kneel down in the street despite his wearing a black tuxedo which clearly showed that he had come off work for lunch and would be returning to work in a few minutes time. "Josh, come with me," Janet said and walked back to the motel. Rosemary was beside her. And in the midst of all the people going about and others talking, Janet heard the sound of instruments as they were being dragged along towards the motel.

With a guitar strapped around him, Josh approached Janet and Rosemary before they could enter the motel.

"I promise I am going to make you the happiest

woman to have ever lived on this earth," Josh started.

"Get us more chairs Rosemary," Janet said and as if she knew what Janet had meant she broke off to some isolated tables in the motel and got three plastic chairs which she brought to the table she and Janet had earlier shared. She tucked the chairs inside the table carefully. Janet sat on hers, Josh flopped on his next to Janet and Rosemary went around the table to sit at the chair opposite Josh but she was startled like everyone at the table. They heard the loud splatter of the musical instruments at the entrance and then footsteps running towards the table.

A man, the one who had been on drums ran behind Rosemary and carefully pulled the chair for her to sit on. "For the beautiful lady," he said. Rosemary appeared charmed and Janet saw her blush.

"Thank you."

"This guitar here--" Josh removed the guitar from his chest and passed it to Janet "Is a symbol of our love. We will look on this day and laugh at this day--"

"Why don't you start with introducing your friends," Janet said, got the guitar and put it on the table. Josh's friends were now sitting down, the one who had pushed the chair for Rosemary sat next to Rosemary and the two couldn't take their eyes off each other. Rosemary smiled at him and he smiled back and she looked away, obviously to remind herself that she was in the company of other people. The other sat next to Josh and opposite his friend.

"Right-- that charming man by Rosemary is Mike, he is an accountant at Crystal hotel and I am his assistant. We went to school together and also account school together. We are the best of friends," Josh said. Rosemary giggled, Mark was whispering something to her.

"How did you know Rosemary?"

"Your parents told me that you had a lovely friend-- a receptionist here and that day you two came at Crystal hotel, I just came to know how lovely she can be," Josh said and held his cheek. "Mike, be careful with that girl. She can slap hard."

"I am sorry," Rosemary apologized.

"Already forgiven-- next, this is my brother Daniel. He plays for Corinth High."

"Corinth High?" Rosemary asked. Janet shook her head to prevent her from talking any longer. She knew where this would be going. But Rosemary didn't pay attention to her and proceeded.

"Yes. Why?" Daniel asked.

"I have a brother there-- Philip Madrin, I think you may know him. He plays soccer for Corinth High also."

"You bet I know him. He was top scorer at the last inter-school tournament."

"Your being into soccer explains why you are so terrible at the keyboard," Janet block in, trying to change the mood of the conversation. And all of them at the table laughed.

"We know we were terrible. I tried to get Josh to back away from his decision. He had it since yesterday but he had ran out of any fresh new ones. But after what happened today, it was worth it. I got to meet Rosemary," Mike said and held the hand of Rosemary. He held it tightly and it seemed as though both of them did not want to let go of each other.

"I was desperate for a song and then I remembered where we met-- At Mathew's concert and from there it was easy," Josh said.

"I am glad that I could help. My brother has not had a girlfriend in years--"

"Dan, I told you that once we got here. You would do both of us a favor and kept quiet."

"Stop being too hard on the boy," Janet said.

"You don't know him," Josh responded.

"So how may I address you?-- Josh's girlfriend?" Daniel asked.

"No. Not too fast. Your brother will have to do better then what he did today for me to be his girlfriend. For now just call me Janet, Josh's friend."

"Wait till we get out of here Dan--"

"What have I done wrong? I was just checking if that terrible performance was enough to win her over-- and apparently it wasn't," Daniel said and laughed. Mike over at Rosemary's side with his hand still locked with Rosemary's, tried hard to contain his laughter but he could no longer hold it in and he too broke out and laughed so hard that everybody on the table stared at him. The only person who wasn't laughing, and Janet felt sorry for him, was Josh. He had hinted that what he had done that day was his best shot and if that hadn't won Janet over, Janet reasoned Josh was lost for what could.

"I will keep the guitar though. It may serve as the symbol of the beginning of our love. Who knows?" Janet said and Josh appeared lighted up again, determined once more. Janet hated to see him gloomy and she was glad that he looked reassured. "Rosemary gets off her shift at 6 p.m.," Janet added.

"That is pretty late. A person should not work so long--" Josh began before he was interrupted.

"Do you girls want to have dinner somewhere downtown?" Mark asked.

"Sure we would love to," Janet said, glad that atleast Mike was sensible enough to know why she had told them of the time Rosemary got off work.

"Then we-- I mean me and Josh the rock star minus Daniel will be here before 6 p.m."

The men got up and left, Daniel protested that he wanted to come also. "You don't get it, it will be a double date. You are not needed tonight," Mike told Daniel. And then there was the dragging of musical instruments and Josh complained, the voices distant now that Janet could hardly make out what they were saying, "Your dinner with your mother will have to be postponed. She has given you the chance to prove yourself tonight. Don't waste it," and the voices, the dragging of the instruments were no longer audible to Janet or Rosemary. When Janet looked at her phone, she found that it was an hour past 12, the men were late and so was Rosemary. She told Rosemary of the time and she hurried to return to her post, she too went to her room but before assuring Rosemary that Rosemary could wear one of her dresses to the date that evening. She went up, she didn't have so many clothes to pick from but she needed to look good that night and she had a task of picking out an outfit for Rosemary as well as herself. She beamed at how stunning the two would look at diner and she went inside her room.

Later that evening, the three got into the car that Janet later found out belonged to Josh, the men had arrived to pick them from the motel in time. And they had been patient enough to wait for Rosemary get ready for the dinner after her shift had been over. Both men exercised a high level of patience at the motel but once they had gotten to the dinner, things turned around and Janet could only wish she hadn't gone there. Mike was a gentleman and treated Rosemary with such care that Janet could almost feel envy. The two seemed as though they knew each other. They connected so well that it would come as a surprise to anyone when they learnt that the two had only met that afternoon. They seemed to laugh at the same jokes. Both were ever happy and when they went on stage to dance at the exquisite restaurant the men had reserved dinner at, they appeared as though they were one. Never had Janet seen anybody complete another as Rosemary and Mike were. But Josh was a different story. In his calm and soft voice he tormented her because he couldn't let even five minutes pass before he could ask Janet if she was now willing to be his girlfriend, when Janet was hesitant, Josh would lament about how he could make her the happiest woman on earth but when Janet expressed more reluctance, he put on a mood and didn't talk to her for minutes. And after he saw that his behavior wasn't helping him at all, he would resume smiling, come closer to Janet and ask her for a dance or something romantic and when both of them would go on stage amongst all those couples who looked to be so much into each other, he would reluctantly hold her close to him and dance with moves which were foreign to Janet and probably anyone on stage. Whilst Janet tried desperately to move in rhythm to the steps she was forced to dance to Josh's moves. Josh would tell her how and what a wonderful couple they made and how everybody in the room was envious of them and he would proceed to ask her to be his girlfriend. Never had Janet seen a man as needy and as desperate as Josh was. And even though he was determined, his determination made her sick to the stomach and by the time their date was over, Janet was sure Josh had asked her to be his girlfriend for more times than she had seen the sun rise in her life. And by the time they pulled off to the motel and she was walking alone to the entrance whilst Josh remained in the car, too moody to escort her in, she understood that he didn't respond too well to rejection or delayment or anything which didn't go in his favor.

Her friend, Rosemary and Mike walked beside her to the entrance, they didn't dare ask her what was going on because they probably knew. When they reached the entrance of the motel, they hugged passionately and surprisingly Rosemary pulled off from the hug and kissed Mike. It was a brief and short kiss but it was filled with love and it had surprisingly caught both of them off-guard because after that brief moment, the two people Janet knew who could joke, laugh, and smile at all times appeared lost for words.

"I will come by tomorrow," Mike finally said in a whisper.

"And I will be waiting for you," Rosemary responded after a few seconds. And both Janet and Rosemary watched mark go. He entered into the car and without Josh hesitating to wave at Janet or say goodbye to her too, he sped off. Rosemary was left starring in the distance. She touched her lips and turned to face Janet.

"I have never felt like I am feeling today."

"That is because you have never being in love before-- tell me why did you tell Mike you wanted to be dropped off here and not at your house--"

"Because I am afraid that if he knows where I stay, this may go faster than it is going."

Early the next morning, Janet and Rosemary yawned into the mirror together. Whilst Rosemary bathed, Janet tuned into the radio and she was glad that Mathew had decided to stay in Canada and was almost done with his tour around Canada. But she was only disappointed that he had decided to cancel his last performance in Timmins. And when she told Rosemary, she too was disappointed but not as much as Janet was.

Rosemary quickly got ready for work and descended down and when she opened the door to the corridor, Janet was disappointed. She expected her to announce that there was another bouquet of flowers on the door from Josh but the absence of the flowers proved that Josh had given up on her. She did not want to tell Rosemary how disappointed she felt but decided it was probably for the best that Josh moved on. She hoped that they would continue to be friends. A love relationship between them had clearly failed and no matter how hard Josh pushed, she doubted she would see him in a different light than the bad impression he had imprinted on her the previous night at dinner. She looked over at Josh's guitar which stood beside her mirror and she smiled at the ugly sounds it made the previous day under the control of Josh. And she decided she definitely wanted to be friends with Josh. So she stepped into the shower, took a quick one, did her make-up and resolved that she would go to Crystal hotel where she planned to reaffirm her interest in a friendship with Josh.

She turned back to look at the guitar once again, it may not have been proof of Josh and her love but it sure was proof of their friendship. A determined and persistent friendship even though he had made noise with the guitar the previous day. Janet had never met anyone with the audacity to disturb a city like Josh had done talentless though he was, just to get the attention of the girl he thought was for him.

She walked to the reception and when she saw that Rosemary was busy there, she proceeded to walk out of the building, resolving to tell Rosemary everything when she returned from Crystal hotel. After several minutes, the cab she had booked pulled over in front of the hotel. Janet went to the gate but as fast as she had gone there was she sent back. Apparently Josh had left word by the gate that she was not welcome to any part of the hotel. And midst laughter from the two guards who opened the gate for her, she knew that there was nothing she could do now and she went back to the road to wait for a cab and moments later she was at Moreal.

When she entered into Moreal, she found Rosemary staring at the entrance dreamly, and Janet knew that unlike the first time she had met her, she was not bored but was thinking about Mike. So almost sure that Rosemary did not see her inspite of her passing right in front of her eyes, Janet proceeded to go up the stairs, she did not want to disturb Rosemary who was lost in thought and clearly happy because she was beaming as she looked at the entrance. Janet only went down at 6 p.m. and what she saw sank her heart. Instead of the dreamy state she had left Rosemary in, she found her pacing up and down clearly waiting for someone, disappointment written all over her face. The receptionist for that shift had already arrived and she was settling down behind her desk. When Janet saw how worried Rosemary was, she was certain she knew what was bothering her. Mike was nowhere to be seen. Janet knew she needed to consul her friend and she walked to her. Immediately Rosemary saw Janet, she wept.

"I knew it was too good to last. I shouldn't have hoped for so much."

"You have the right to hope for so much," Janet said whilst she caressed Rosemary's head. Rosemary suddenly pulled away from her embrace.

"I rather be alone."

"No. I am here for you. We are friends, remember?"

"I am going home," Rosemary said and left.

"I can't let you go in this condition--" Janet said but Rosemary was already gone.

The receptionist stared at Janet with an interest like she wanted to know what was going on but Janet ignored her and went back to her room. Mike's decision to back down from his promise to come see Rosemary or on their new found relationship had Josh deeply imprinted in it and Janet knew why. He had after all said that the two were the best of friends, so he must have told him to quit seeing Rosemary just like he had given up on her. Janet felt bad, a lovely relationship had been ended too early because of her. She had a day left to live in Moreal and she was sad she had been the one who had been responsible for her only-friend-in-Timmin's heart break.

When she was inside her room, she failed to sleep. That day she even failed to tune on the radio. She was worried about what her friend must have been going through at that moment. She remembered about how happy Rosemary was at lunch and at dinner the previous day and she was willing to propose a compromise to Josh. He needed to stop controlling his friend and let him be happy and Rosemary and him surely looked happy. She could only imagine what Josh had told him. Maybe he told him to choose between their friendship or Rosemary and Mike was stupid enough to choose the friendship he shared with Josh.

She didn't have Josh's phone number so there was no way she could contact him. She therefore resolved that she was going to try her luck once more at Crystal hotel and get Josh to back away from something as beautiful as what she had seen the previous day between Rosemary and Mike. With that thought, she switched off the lights and forced herself to sleep.

Early the next day, her last day at Moreal, she stepped into the shower and washed herself for a long time probably because she was considering what to do if the guards at Crystal laughed at her again and forced her to go back. She did not need to fail that time because it was her last day in Timmins and her last chance to fix a relationship which had been broken because of her.

She wore her blue dress, got a matching purse and matching heels and was soon getting down the stairs. When she emerged to the reception, what she saw down there moved her heart. She had only seen something so beautiful on television and it had happened to her once but because she did not love the history teacher that time, she was sure it did not feel the same as what Rosemary was feeling down there.

Continuing to slowly descend the stairs, she clearly saw that Mike was kneeling in front of Rosemary and holding a ring to her. And Janet had to do nothing for that to happen. The two truly loved each other. Janet approached the two immediately Rosemary had said "I do." When Rosemary saw Janet come to them, she ran to her and hugged her very tightly.

"He has propose marriage and I have accepted."

"That is good but it is not me you must be hugging right now. Look at the poor man. He is still kneeling," Janet whispered to Rosemary who quickly realized how stupid she had been and quickly went to Mike, she pulled him up and when he was up, she kissed him longer and deeper than the last time. A sight which was wonderful to see and to romantic to ignore. The couple kept at this for a minute and when Rosemary pulled away from the kiss, Mike pulled her into another which also lasted for a minute which was as romantic if not passionate than the last one. Janet had to remind them that she was there.

Mike finally pulled away from Rosemary and stared at Janet.

"Thank you for bringing us together. If it wasn't for you, I couldn't have met her."

"Anytime," Janet responded.

"I am sorry that you and Josh didn't work out though. I saw his behavior that day at dinner and I am sorry he acted that way."

"It is not your fault. Don't blame yourself."

"Oh, before I forget. . ." Mike said and went over to the reception desk. Behind the desk, he pulled out two red high slippers, the ones that Janet had worn at Mathew's concert. Janet had forgotten about them because she knew that she would never find them. "Josh gave me these. He no longer wants anything to do with you."

"I am not surprised," Janet said and reached for her slippers from Mike and immediately she had retrieved them from him, Mike returned to Rosemary and held Rosemary's hand, the one he had pushed the ring into and the two giggled.

Mike then stared back at Janet shyly.

"May I borrow her?"

"Yes sure, but for how long?"

“A day?” Mike said, Rosemary blushed.

“Yes sure if that is okay with her boss. Remember, she works here.”

“But this can not wait-- Rosemary call your boss, make up an excuse to go out and have someone fill in your position and later I will personally mail the motel your resignation letter.”

“Why do you want me to resign?” Rosemary asked.

“Because we are moving to the U.S. I have been transferred there at a newly opened sister company of Crystal hotel--”

“I just can’t leave this place, I have family here.”

“I know that, that is why I borrowed you for a day. We will go to your parents, ask them for your hand in marriage and if we are lucky, get married at Crystal hotel-- and as for your job you will have a better one in Florida, you will be a receptionist at the hotel I have been transferred to and it is better than Crystal hotel.”

“Really?”

“Yes,” Mike responded and held Rosemary very tightly. Rosemary appeared shocked and she held Mike and slowly caressed him. It was as though she was happy but couldn’t believe that was happening to her.

“You two are so adorable. You have my permission. Go and be happy-- Rosemary just give me your boss’s contact number and I will handle everything,” Janet said, half in tears and half excited.

“It is in the blue address book under the desk.”

“let us go already,” Mike said and pulled Rosemary

along and sped towards the entrance.

Janet walked to the reception desk before she stopped and stared in Rosemary and Mike's direction. And before they could disappear from sight, Janet called out to Mike.

"Mike!"

Mike peeped back to the reception. Rosemary was the one now pulling him. "You will love my mom--she's so adorable," Rosemary said, she had obviously shaken herself from her shock and was now loving what was about to happen to her.

"How is Josh?" Janet inquired.

"Devastated. Heart broken but busy than ever. He will get over what happened especially with the promotion-- he is now accountant, taking over my job and he is busy, everybody at Crystal hotel is busy with the arrival of Mathew from his tour around Canada. He is scheduled to stay there for some days."

"Mathew is at Crystal?"

"Yes," Mike responded. Rosemary pulled him "Lets go!" she said.

"Give me Josh's number. I want to apologize to him for whatever has happened."

"Sure." and Josh proceeded to say out loud the digits to Josh's phone number which Janet hurriedly typed in her phone and when he said the last digit was he pulled away from view by Rosemary. Janet heard the two couple giggle along as they went along. She composed herself and saved Josh's number in her phone, she went behind Rosemary's desk and searched for the blue file she had talked about where her boss's address was.

Talking to Rosemary's boss, Janet reasoned, would give her ample time to clearly reason on what she was about to do. She found Rosemary's boss's number and when she told him about what had happened, he turned out to be understanding. He also offered that she stay at the reception for that day whilst he considered the many applications for Rosemary's job. He however demanded that he wanted to talk to Rosemary in person and Janet assured him that Rosemary would be back before 7 p.m. and he agreed to be at the motel before that time.

Next, she called Josh and the phone continued to ring. And after some time, it was cut. She called again and it rang and finally Josh answered.

"Isn't it enough that you rejected me in person?" Josh spoke into the phone.

"What are you talking about?" Janet sobbed into the phone. She had never heard Josh speak at her with such vileness and distaste before even when she was hesitant at dinner about being his girlfriend he had maintained his cool and retried but to no luck. "I never said no. I only told you to wait."

"I know when I am rejected. I am hanging up, I have nothing to do with you anymore."

"You give up too fast. What you don't realize is that I also like you," Janet said and cut off the phone call. Josh tried to call but Janet ignored his calls, wiped her tears and concentrated on the job she had been assigned by Rosemary's boss. The phone rang another three times before it went silent for several minutes and Josh never called again.

However after thirty minutes, Janet heard tire screeches from an over-speeding vehicle. She watched in horror as it almost crushed into the motel's entrance. And surprisingly, out of the car came Josh, he ran to her and behind her desk. He was ecstatic, his tie was loose but he was still smartly dressed.

"Did you mean it?" Josh asked. He kissed Janet on her forehead and was going down. "I love you Janet." And he kissed her on the lips.

"And I am ready to be your girlfriend," Janet said. Josh held tightly Janet's hands, he brought both of them to his lips and kissed them passionately before he stared deep into her eyes.

"You have made me the happiest man in-- Why am I telling you this alone?--" he released her hands and ran towards his car. Janet watched him go, she was dumbfounded about what was on his mind but she did not stop him. She loved to see him that happy.

Josh climbed on top of his car, undid the two remaining buttons of his tuxedo and released both his hands in a gesture as if he wanted the sunshine which was beginning to shine to wash all over him, and then he exclaimed "Thank you! If not for you people I could have never won her over. You did not chase me when I gave a poor solenade but encouraged me on, now look at me! She has agreed to be my girlfriend. You were all witnesses to my poor attempts at making an impression and for that I bow! I bow!" he said and systematically bowed down two times. Janet was more than impressed, she wanted to scream at him to come down but she marveled into what Josh was doing and she had to admit that no one other than Josh had done that for her ever. She stared at him and smiled. "She has made me the happiest man alive and I promise all of you today that I will make her the happiest woman to have ever lived!" This was followed by an applause. It was clear that his antics had impressed the crowd and had gathered people once again. "Josh and Janet are now a love story. She is now my girlfriend. No, no. . . How stupid of me! A girlfriend status doesn't suit her, she deserves to be a wife!" and he jumped down from his car and ran towards the reception desk.

Janet wondered what he was up to but before she could protest, she had already been held tightly by the hand and was been dragged along. She remembered how Mike had dragged Rosemary along and she smiled and then giggled. Josh took this as encouragement and proceeded to the car, he climbed the bonnet of the car and offered his hands to Janet. Janet stared around at the bemused crowd and couldn't refuse Josh. She reluctantly brought up her hands and Josh slowly pulled her up and when she was on the bonnet, Josh climbed the top of the car and urged her on. He pulled her up and when they were both up for the whole people to see, and when her heart was beating so fast in her heart in anticipation of what Josh would do next, did Josh go down on his knees. Janet brought her hands to her open mouth and clasp it.

"Janet, in the presence of all these people, make me the happiest man than I already am. Where's the ring," Josh said and searched rampantly in his pockets both jacket and pants that it sent a melodious laughter from the crowd below and up on the buildings staring down. "When you are lucky like me, things happen quickly that you don't know what will happen next. I did not know this would ever happen so I did not buy a ring but all in due time. My fairest Janet, will you marry me?"

Janet brought Josh up and hugged him.

"All in due time Josh," Janet said but Josh did not mind and pulled away from the tight embrace. He planted a kiss on Janet which seemed to have gone on forever, and especially with the people cheering them and clapping them on that Josh was encouraged and kissed her so passionately that Janet was convinced Josh was in love and not just some passing whim which she had feared it would be.

Later that day, when Josh had nicely packed his car, and the crowd had dispersed, Janet and Josh talked all day. She got to know a lot about Josh and she told most about herself to Josh too like what foods she liked since he already knew what music she enjoyed, she told him what she liked to do every night before she slept. Since he already knew about her parents, she told him about her job and her two good friends in Saute Ste Marie. And Josh told her everything about him that she had a hard time remembering it all. He told her everything including the time he had lost his first tooth.

They ate lunch together, and for the first time Janet saw that Josh was a charming man too and when he was not trying to desperately get something, he too could be lovable. In the middle of their meal Josh received a phone call from Mike telling him to arrange for an impromptu wedding at Crystal hotel. Janet was happy that Rosemary's mother had agreed to the wedding.

"What a nice way to say goodbye," Josh said before he made several calls to the hotel for other people to arrange the wedding. He claimed that there was no way he would leave his princess alone to work. Janet insisted that he should go but he was stubborn and stayed. He worked with Janet at the desk or was it just to ploy to continuously be rubbing against her and blush. He continually held her in between customer visits that Janet could almost swear he appeared cuter when he was in love.

Finally he lamented that he did not want to miss his best friend's wedding and Janet realized that neither did she want to miss her friend, Rosemary's. He offered to bring down Daniel at the motel to take over so that the two of them would go to Crystal hotel and wait for the ceremony to begin which was scheduled for 6 p.m. in the evening but Janet blatantly refused, there was no way that she would run the place like it belonged to her, so she phoned the other receptionist, she was happy at the news that Rosemary would be married and wanted to go to the wedding also but she finally understood and agreed to come down and take over earlier than usual.

With Josh hugging her from behind, she called Rosemary's boss. She explained everything to him and he understood. He agreed to make it to the wedding and when she was done talking to Rosemary's boss, she held Josh's hair from behind her.

"Won't you let me work properly?"

"Never."

"What did he think when you repeatedly breathed down heavily on the phone?"

"I don't know. I don't care-- lets go already."

"We have to wait for the next receptionist-- and here she comes," Janet said when she saw her walk into the reception. Janet then handed over to Josh the red high heels she had got from Mike.

"A symbol of our first day together," Josh said and sniffed on them. "I wanted to keep them. May I keep them?"

"No. Take them to my room," Janet said and gave him the room keys. Josh rushed up the stairs and within five minutes he was back down.

"I hope you didn't throw them on the bed or on the floor," Janet protested when she considered how fast Josh had gone to her room.

"That is for you to find out," he said and before he could pull Janet's hand, he quickly said to the receptionist, "thank you for filling in on such a short notice." And the two of them were gone.

Within a few minutes they were at Crystal hotel. When the two guards at the hotel saw her hand in hand with Josh, they said, "What a love story!" and they broke out laughing as usual.

"Don't mind them, they are always like that," Josh said.

"I noticed," Janet said.

When they were inside the glamorous hotel, they found everything had been set and only a few touches remained. Josh and Janet worked hand in hand to make sure everything was ready before 6 p.m. And at close to 6 the guests started arriving, she met Josh's parents and Mike's parents. She met Rosemary's mother. Her father was late and she also met Rosemary's only brother and he looked so handsome especially when he wore that tuxedo. Daniel also came and right before the couple would arrive, Rosemary's boss arrived. He talked to Janet for a little and was discussing about giving Rosemary her benefits considering how loyal and hardworking she had been to him for all those years she worked for him.

When the couple came in, the first people they saw

were Janet and Josh standing side by side and holding each others arms that both Mike and Rosemary instantly knew that things had worked out between the two.

Rosemary went to hug Janet and whispered to her, "I knew he was the guy for you the moment I saw him." And over at her side Janet saw Mike shake Josh's hand in a gesture to congratulate him that it almost seemed it was Josh and Janet's wedding and not the two's.

After the wedding, Josh unveiled the surprise last act he had concealed from Janet and everybody else. It was Mathew, he looked refreshed and he only performed one song for the venue and as Janet sat close to Josh with the couple directly opposite them on the huge table, she had to remind herself that Josh was her reality and Mathew her fantasy.

"Do you like the surprise?" Josh asked her and held her hand under the table.

"Yes, you are the best," Janet responded and looked at Rosemary who smiled as if to reassure her that she had made the best choice.

Chapter Three

When they had bid their friends farewell and goodbye and got the address of the house they would be living in Florida, they watched their car go and when it was well hidden from view, Josh turned to Janet and depressingly said, "I am sad that they are not the only ones who have to go--"

"What do you mean?"

"You are leaving tomorrow too-- I promised your father that I would personally take you home."

"And both my parents are expecting you. What did you tell them for them to like you so much?"

"I have my ways," Josh said and looked innocently at the dark sky and away from Janet, he had both his hands tucked inside his trouser pockets.

"Look at you boast," Janet said teasingly and punched Josh on the shoulder, he smiled and looked at her.

"Since you are leaving tomorrow, I want to make the most of this night-- we may have dinner with my family and you may sleep over at my house--"

"I would rather stay here. Besides, I don't want to go home yet."

"Meaning?"

"Book me a room at Crystal hotel, I want to stay a few more days."

"Why would you want that?"

"For me to get to know you more, or am I asking for much?"

"It's decided then. I will book you a room here and after dinner with my parents I will escort you back here."

"The dinner will have to wait. I am tired from all that wedding preparations for Rosemary that all I want is to get my things at Moreal, come here and sleep like an angel you claim I am."

"Yes you are and I won't allow you to go to Moreal. Stay here and rest. I will go down there and get your things."

But when Janet thought of the two pants hanging in the bathroom and a few breast holders she had left lying on top of the clothes in her suitcase, she decided she would be too embarrassed to let Josh see those. There was no way she wanted him to see those yet, she would be sharing intimate moments of her to him too soon. So she insisted that she wanted to personally retrieve her things and when Josh insisted that he would do it for her, she told him she wanted to thank Rosemary's shift receptionist for what she had done for them that day and Josh let her go especially when she told him to be in charge of organizing her room at Crystal hotel. They went back to Crystal hotel where Josh gave her his car keys and in Josh's car, she drove to Moreal.

She went into Moreal, got her things, thanked the receptionist, and drove back to Crystal hotel and when she entered into the room Josh had booked for her, she still found him organizing it. The room was expensive, everything there looked exquisite, the bed and bed linens were exquisite, the big flat screened television opposite the bed looked wonderful too and she could almost bet it was connected to cable. When she entered the room, Josh looked at her, he was holding a couple of pants and bras in his hands that made Janet blush, she had prevented him from going to Moreal because she didn't want him to look at her underwear but she now found him holding others which she was sure he had bought for her.

"How do you like the room?"

"The room is superb-- but what is that you are holding in your hands?"

"I think you know what this is."

"I think you are overstepping your boundaries."

"Come here."

Janet hesitantly approached Josh, she did not know what he was up to. Josh walked towards the window. He opened it and stepped outside on the balcony. "Do you smell the fresh breeze-- we have a huge pool here--

and I did tell you I loved water and swimming-- now tell me miss Josh, how is it you are going to go swimming with that dress or any of your dresses?"

Josh made a good point. She had also told him that even though she swam rarely, she too did know how to swim and therefore Janet knew that there was no way she could avoid water for very long whilst she lived at Crystal and especially with Josh as her boyfriend.

"I have bought everything-- red, blue, pink bikinis, you will choose the ones which are comfortable for you but I think all of them would look good on you. I have also acquired some extra clothes for you. I want to show you, for the few days you will live here-- I have told your parents 5, I told them you wanted to see some sights in Timmins-- for those five days I will show you to my friends, family and take you throughout Timmins. Just you wait. You are going to have the time of your life in Timmins that we will go back to Saute Ste Marie to only ask for your hand in marriage."

"I told you in due time."

"Yes I know," Josh said and walked back into the room, Janet walked inside too. He threw the pants, bras, bikinis in his hands on the bed and kissed Janet. Janet held him by the head and slowly caressed his head when he wanted to go any further.

"I said all in due time."

"I know-- I love you Janet."

"I know."

"I will leave you alone now. Get comfortable and I will be here first thing tomorrow morning." Josh then walked slowly to the door and before he could open it, he turned back and stared in the direction of Janet "Sleep well, wonderful dreams. Dream about me?"

"Goodnight Josh," Janet said and Josh was out of her room.

Early the next morning, Janet was woken up by the ringtone of her phone. And when she reached out for her phone she knew instantly that it was Josh who had called her. He did promise that he would be at the hotel the first thing that morning. So Janet reasoned that he was outside her room or something. But when she answered the phone, with her eyes half closed because of the sleep in her eyes, it was not Josh's voice she heard but her mother's.

"Goodmorning mother," Janet said.

"Goodmorning."

"Why call so early in the morning?"

"Because you have somehow forgotten we exist. You don't call anymore. I am guessing you are having such a good time there in Timmins."

"Yes mother. How is father?"

"Don't change the subject-- We may like your new boyfriend but don't think of doing anything funny with him before marriage--"

"Are we going to start with this conversation again?" Janet asked whilst she sat upright now.

"I was just checking-- You may be older but you

are still our daughter and we have values--"

"Okay mother, I get it and I promise."

"Promise what?"

"No sex before marriage."

"Good."

"Greet father for me when he gets back from work."

"What-- Is he there? Did he hear--"

"Yes my dear and I couldn't be more proud of my daughter," Janet's father said on phone. Janet was embarrassed that he had heard her speak to her mother about sex, but he was still on the line and she struggled to find the right words to say next, what she was sure of was that she would tell off her mother when she went home about what she had just put her through.

"Uh-- Good morning Sir?"

"She's embarrassed and shy. You shouldn't have told her that and you shouldn't have put her on loudspeaker--" Janet heard her father tell her mother.

"She did!?" Janet exclaimed on the phone.

"Finish talking to her and tell her to greet that fine young man for me. I have to rush for work," Janet's father said to her mother and then she heard a door open and close.

"Are you still on the line honey?" Janet's mother asked her after a few seconds had past.

"I am no longer talking to you," Janet said and ended their call.

She then scrolled through her phone, she had a lot

of messages and all of them were from Josh. They were similar to the angel note he had once sent her alongside the flowers that she just skimmed through them, uninterested and proceeded to delete them one at a time. When she finished, she threw her phone on the bed and went to the shower. She was half way through her bath when she heard a knock on the door and then the door swing slowly open. She was sure that have been Josh who had come into her room.

"Just a minute Josh!" she exclaimed and tried to bath fast.

"May I come there. . . I promise I won't look."

"Don't even think about it," Janet said. It took her about thirty minutes to completely bath and when she was out she felt refreshed, all the exhaustion from the previous day gone. When she opened the door from her bathroom to her room, she found Josh sitting on her bed with a bouquet of flowers and he had nothing but a boxer on him.

"What are you doing?"

"Oh. . . You are finally out," Josh said and got off the bed and went near Janet.

"Not a step closer"

"Or you will call the police?" Josh asked and laughed. Obviously he had remembered that day when they had met for the second time in the guard room and he now found what she had said funny. But Janet was not kidding. She could only imagine what Josh must have been thinking when he came to her room in nothing but boxers and he should have been someone holding a respectable position at the hotel? "Flowers for my angel?" he said and gave the flowers over to Janet which she reluctantly got from him. "It is a lovely day for a swim. Don't you agree?"

"Weren't you recently promoted. Are you not supposed to be working?"

"Yes and I got here very early. I did most of the work--"

"It is still morning."

"I know and the water is especially lovely."

"I--"

"I won't take 'no' for an answer."

"I will join you soon."

"I can wait-- I promise I won't look."

"Don't be stupid."

"Alright you win. Finish picking up your favorite bikini and I will wait for you by the pool. If you take too long, you may find me in the water."

"Just go."

"I love you." And Josh disappeared from sight.

Janet went over to the dressing mirror and made sure her hair lay securely to the back. She applied a little lotion on her body and when she was done, she looked over the bikinis Josh had got her and she finally settled for a pink bikini which just fit her properly. She knew that day when she would have to go swimming with Josh would come but she didn't know that it would be that soon. So she wore it properly and before she could change her mind, she went out of the room.

Josh, when he saw her, couldn't be more happy. As she approached him, he smiled and when she looked at him securely in the eyes, he blushed and tried to look away as though he was doing something wrong by starring at her like that.

"I thought you wouldn't come. You look extremely beautiful, if that is even possible, by the way-- come with me, hold my hand and I will show you a technique I recently learned," Josh said as he reached out for Janet's hand whilst he continued to sit by the edge of the swimming pool.

When Janet reached for his hand, Josh dived into the water. The water was cold and it took a minute before Janet got accustomed to it. They turned and somersaulted in the water together. They took twists into every direction of the pool together and Josh kissed her many times in the water that Janet had lost count. They splashed water at each other, laughed whilst both of them couldn't come of the water though exhausted they were, Janet had discovered that she loved swimming as much as Josh did and they swam hand in hand, from one side of the pool to the other side. From deep under to the top where Josh threw her up in the air where she got to take in the air and down she came down. At that moment she was happy that she had forgotten why she had come to Crystal hotel in the first place. Until whilst Josh threw her up, for the fifth time, in the air from their dive under did she see him. Time had gone and it was close to 12 p.m. she did not know when he had gotten there but she couldn't mistake that it was him. He sat their with a friend of his, Janet had seen on the drums and they were staring at both her and Josh with a look of amazement and mesmerization. And Janet knew she had to make her move or she would never get such an opportunity again. So she told Josh she wanted to rest and Josh reluctantly agreed.

Leading the way, Janet swam with Josh closely behind him in the direction of the man she wanted to desperately talk to, the rock musician, Mathew himself.

She got out of the water and ran to Mathew. Mathew looked about the chair he sat on, shocked at what was happening and so did his friend who was close by him. Josh behind got out of the water and exhaustively lay on the edges of the pool, though he too stared in the direction where Janet had gone, he too looked surprised at what Janet was doing but not as surprised as Mathew was.

"Mathew, Mathew, I can't believe I am standing in front of you now--" Janet said when she came a few inches from him.

"Great, another fan. Martin, dude, deal with her. I will be in my room-- Why can't I ever get a little peace and quiet. Clearly this place has also failed to provide me that--" Mathew said and got up his chair, he was about to leave but Janet held him by the hand and before Mathew's friend could detach her from him, she kissed him. His supple lips on hers felt like a dream, his heavy breathe on her nostril's was indeed any girl's fantasy but that moment didn't last long because Martin did separate her from him. But even though she was no longer kissing the famous rock musician, she still held him by the hands whilst Martin tried desperately to pull her away from him.

"You don't understand Mathew. My name is Janet. Not only am I your biggest fan, I am also in love with you."

"What?!-- This girl has clearly lost it Martin. Take her off me-- And girl, whoever you are--"

"I believe she said she was Janet."

"I don't care-- just take her off!-- You. Go back to your boyfriend. You should have some dignity," Mathew said, bet her hands off him and stormed off, Martin closely behind him.

Janet knelt down, tears rolling from her eyes, she had never been this desperate before.

"You don't understand. He's not my boyfriend. I love you Mathew, I traveled a long distance just to be with you. I only love you--" But Mathew had by now gone so far from her. He took a turn and disappeared from view. Janet continued weeping and when she looked behind, she saw Josh now sitted, looking shocked than anyone she had ever seen in her life. She got up, still weeping uncontrollably, she had never been rejected before and humiliated like she had been that day, she got up and ran to the hotel and into her room which she securely locked, knowing fully well that Josh would come to her room any time to disturb her, to demand answers but she was in no mood to entertain him anymore. Her love had just rejected her. She couldn't have been more depressed in her entire life.

But Josh never came that day. Janet slept on her bed in her wet bikini and tears seemed not to stop coming out of her for the entire day. She never ate that day and she also didn't know when she had slept off because when she awoke it was already morning and she was famished.

She decided that she was going to go home. She stepped into the shower and as hot water gushed down her body, they were mixed with tears which had started streaming down once more when she replayed images of her rejection the previous night. Rejection hurt and now she knew it. Heart breaks could be painful and true love was painful, she tried to control herself but she couldn't and by the time she had turned off the shower, her tears had still not ceased from streaming down her cheeks. She thought of drying her hair but it was of no use. She did not feel like it. She thought of applying make-up but she reasoned: who was she trying to impress? She did not care how she looked, she would take the next train to Saute Ste Marie looking scruffy with her skin lotion-free. Mathew didn't find her beautiful enough to love her back so she didn't care what anybody on the streets, on the train or in the neighborhood would think about her appearance when she would go back. So she rapped around her body a huge towel and stepped out of the shower and when she heard the door bell ring, she reasoned that must have been room service. She was hungry and she wouldn't brush room service away, so she hurried for the door.

But she walked too fast that she did not realize that her wrapped up towel had now become loose when she opened her door and when she did open her door she did not see room service there but Mathew with his guitar. She couldn't contain her excitement, she screamed and cupped her hand on her mouth but no sooner did she do that, her towel fell off her and she was in display for Mathew to look her over. And before she realized what was going on to pick up the towel, Mathew had already entered her room. And he was dangerously close to her.

"Wow," he said and continued to walk inside, he dropped his guitar and it made a loud thud when it hit the ground. Janet was confused, there standing in front of her was the man she loved but she never wanted him to see her like that, so she walked back even farther from the towel. "Is it true what you had said. That you love me. . . traveled a long distance to tell me so?" Mathew asked before he lowered down his head and kissed Janet. And even though his breath and taste had a sour feel like he had been smoking, she still couldn't deny that was the most magical moment for her. She kissed him back and nodded. Mathew continued to kiss her and she returned his kiss passionately whilst moving closer to her bed. Mathew quickly removed his clothes and before she knew it, Mathew's hand was on her chest, their bodies were under the thin wet white bed linens and they had just had sex.

Janet caressed Mathew's blond hair as she could not believe what had just happened. It had been the first time that she had sex and it was a magical one.

Mathew looked at her and deep into her eyes. It was as though he too didn't believe what had happened had happened.

"Did you mean it. Do you love me?" Mathew asked unbelievably. He looked shocked and Janet didn't know why.

"Yes I do. I meant every word I said yesterday," she said and Mathew reached for her head and the two kissed passionately again. And in the midst of their kiss, Janet stared slightly at the opened door. They had not closed it and what she saw sank her heart. She saw Josh, he had just seen everything which had happened in there. And before Janet could scream his name to explain things, did he go away from the door post. He looked so white as if he did not have blood in him. This time, Janet knew she had to talk to him.

"Josh wait!" but he had already gone, running through the corridor.

"I thought you said he wasn't your boyfriend," Mathew said, he also had apparently seen Josh go.

"No he is not. He is just a good friend."

"You better be telling me the truth. Because if he is your boyfriend, then we have done a terrible thing to him."

"Well, he thought that he was my boyfriend."

"What?" Mathew got up and dressed "I have to find him-- I can't believe you have put me through this-- What we did was wrong," Mathew said and left the room.

However, Janet did not consider it wrong. What they had just done felt so right despite her values and morals and moreover that she had done it with the man whom she fancied and loved, nothing could have been more magical than that moment and she got off her bed with linens still in place and went to the mirror, she looked at her reflection and she radiated with happiness. She was so happy that she proceeded to dry her hair and put lotion on her face, hands, and legs.

Never did she know that love could make her beam like that before. Finally she and Mathew were a story despite how fantastic he had appeared to be at first. She combed her hair, she knew she had done Josh wrong but she was sure he would understand and it was to him that she planned on going to explain things.

After an hour, right after she had her breakfast, she locked the door and went looking for Josh. She went first to his office, he had shown her his office when they had worked together for the wedding the previous day, and it was there that Janet was sure she would find Josh. So going up, through the elevator, to the third floor, to Josh's office, she found it locked. And she had nowhere else left to look for him. She descended and was on her way out of the hotel, she came to the guards by the guard house, but they too expressed ignorance on Josh's whereabouts, they just told her that they had opened the gate for the 'young man' an hour ago and Josh had driven out looking very furious that he hadn't even said 'hello' to any of them as he habitually did.

"Couple's first fight?" one guard asked.

"You may say that," Janet answered and turned back to walk in the direction of the hotel.

One her way to her room, Janet met Mathew, who was coming from her room, he had obviously found it closed. And upon seeing the rock star Janet still couldn't contain her excitement, she stood frozen at the sight of him. She could not believe that an hour ago, she had shared an experience so magical with him that Rosemary couldn't have believed it even if it had come from Mathew himself.

"I have been looking for you babe-- Come with me, I wanna show you something'"

"You mean it?" Janet said and reached out for Mathew's stretched out hand. Mathew held her and the two walked out of the hotel.

"'There is no way I could have forgotten an amazing fuck like you-- I meant lady. . . lady-- Am so geared up baby!" Mathew said.

"I can see that-- So where are you taking me?"

"To make your trip worth it, I am Mathew after all-- wow!-- we are going to the last concert baby. . . wow!-- we are going to rock!. . . and. . . roll!" Mathew said, a couple of people coming into the hotel looked at him. Janet wanted to be embarrassed at Mathew's behavior but she was too happy to. She could not believe all her dreams were coming true. She would go to Mathew's concert and not just stand in the front lines but wherever important people, people close to Mathew watched his shows from. And from what she had heard Mathew say, it was obvious that he had decided to perform once again in Canada.

"Where are we going?" Janet asked when they arrived at the hotel's parking lot and were going into the secluded part of the lot where a black van with all tinted glasses was which Janet could have sworn she had seen somewhere.

"Right here in Timmins, my last show here, let's get this over with!" Mathew said and opened the black van for Janet, Janet got in and Mathew got in after her, pushing her all the way to the side as he sat where she had sat. When he closed the door, the driver started the van and it sped through the hotel's yard and when it came to the gate, Mathew opened the window, released his head and screamed in the direction of the guard house, "Mathew! Open the damn gate!"

And the gate opened but in time for Janet to hear one of the guards say, "Hey Jod, it's that weed smoking american." and the car passed the gate and Janet remembered that it was here that she had seen that car and she confirmed that it was the same car. Mathew had been there when she first came to Crystal and probably was going out for his tour around Canada.

"Where's your crew?" Janet asked as soon as Mathew lowered his head back inside and the windows closed again.

"They always go ahead of me. Here, meet my manager," Mathew slightly stood up and slapped the head of the man beside the driver in the front seat, Janet hadn't recognized he had been there all along. "Name's stephen Mahon-- stupid name, right?" and the man, in his early fifties turned around and smiled at Janet.

"Nice to meet you miss Janet-- Martin told me all about you."

"He did?" Janet said as she became embarrassed after remembering what she had done the previous day. She recalled having to beg Mathew to reconsider her. And she did not want to have that impression on his manager.

"Oh yes."

"Then it's my pleasure to meet you too," Janet said shyly and extended her hand which Mathew's manager caught in time, still maintaining his smile. They shook hands like that for a minute and everything returned to normal in the car. The manager kept quiet and stared at the road, the car sped along. Janet relaxed in her seat.

Everything was quiet in the car except Mathew who kept screaming yoo's and yeepee's for as long as they were on the road and when they arrived at the back of the concert Janet had been to the first day, Mathew was the first to get out. "Let's do this!" he said and ran into the concert. Janet was left standing awkwardly with the manager, not knowing what to do.

"Let's not just stand here, let us go inside," the manager said and Janet, folding her hands in shock of what Mathew was in person, walked inside also.

Once inside, Janet saw Mathew's crew backstage, she walked excitedly to them. Mathew was busy jumping up and down when she approached them. And behind the stage, Janet could hear a lot of people chanting about and she knew that the venue was already packed and waiting for the show to begin, waiting for Mathew to arrive.

Janet came near Mathew but he was too excited to notice her, he continued to jump perhaps in preparation for show but Janet needed him to introduce her to his friends. She stood there, the crew members starring at her, she felt awkward until Martin said something.

"Guys, this is that crazy girl I told you about," Martin said, Janet couldn't feel more embarrassed. She smiled and waved at them all.

"Hey!" and then Mathew noticed her.

"Martin--Gerald--Scunka, meet my new babe," he said and they broke out laughing.

"Who was your old babe?" Scunka asked and all of them laughed, Mathew obviously feeling embarrassed continued as if to defend himself.

"You people just jealous cause she's beautiful and a good fuck too." everybody stopped laughing and it was the time for Janet to feel embarrassed. Her cheeks burned with embarrassment and she looked down, all excitement of being there gone and as if she couldn't feel any more worse, Mathew's friends came to her and greeted her one by one. She had to struggle to look them in the eyes whilst she greeted them.

"My name is Scunka-- my real name is Marshall C. Delafyente McDonaldo Lindolf but Mathew named me Scunka and I have been called that ever since. I can't wait to know what name Mathew is going to give you," he said. He looked very young and worc clothes loosely, he could have suited the hipper gangster homeless guys of New York and Janet doubted his story was any further from that. But strangely she liked him and felt free with him than any of the two friends of Mathew she had just greeted and she therefore spoke freely with him, intending to ask him what was on her mind ever since the hotel.

"Is Mathew always like this?"

"Yes he is a piece of shit but talented. Never seen him normal since I joined the band-- wanna join us?"

"I don't know."

"It is fun on-stage. Don't worry you will do nothing, just provide backup vocals for Mathew. I heard you are a huge fan of his so I am guessing you know most of his songs."

"All of them."

"Good then."

"I don't know about this--" Mathew's manager said but it was too late, they had already gone on stage, following the band and immediately took her position at one of the back microphones, closely behind Scunka and at the microphones she found two more people there, a lady and a man, she guessed that they too were there to provide backup vocalization for Mathew. Janet stared at the people, she had never been on stage before and more so in front of those people, a magnitude of them. They suddenly became unruly, they became wild and Janet instantly knew why. Mathew had just ran on stage and the show began.

On stage, she rocked and rolled and she had a great time, all did that when the show was over, it ended in the late afternoons, all members of the band were exhausted but happy. However none of them looked as exhausted as Mathew looked. Mathew, Janet, and Mahon, Mathew's manager were the first to leave the concert and they entered into the black van they had come in with. Mathew was helped inside by the driver, and the manager took his seat besides the driver. Janet sat with Mathew and a concern for him emerged. He looked so dejected and opposed to the hipper sensitive self she had earlier seen him, he looked down-spirited and almost dead. He lay on Janet's lap with his eyelids half closed. Janet looked at him and then at his manager who seemed not to care, as though what was happening in the back seat was too normal to notice.

"What is wrong with him all of the sudden?-- he was happy when we came here and on stage." But the manager didn't answer any of her questions. They traveled in silence and when they came to Crystal hotel, the car rolled in and went straight for the parking lot, where a space was specially reserved for it. Janet, Mahon, and the driver got off the car leaving Mathew temporarily inside.

"Go back to your room," Mahon said.

"I can't just leave him like this," Janet protested, opened the door to Mathew's side and tried to pull him out of the vehicle.

"We will handle him."

"I said I won't--"

"Driver lets go. Lets see if she can support his weight," Mahon said now furious at Janet and the two men left.

Janet struggled to pull Mathew off the vehicle and when she did she struggled to support him to walk. He was half unconscious and Mahon and the driver were walking too fast out of the parking lot and Janet didn't know the room Mathew stayed in. So she gathered up all her strength and carefully walked with Mathew and helped him take steps and walked in the direction of the departing Mahon.

"He needs a doctor!" Janet called out, Mahon

ignored her and turned a corner. She hurried and in time to see him enter an elevator just at the back entrance of the hotel. And just before it could close, Janet carried Mathew in with her. " For his manager, you seem like you don't care for him."

"Look at her talk-- You came today and you tell me how to treat my client?"

"Stephen, dude I am weak--" Mathew said.

"I know," Mahon compassionately said.

"help me to my bedroom. Please my. . . bedroom-- don't let her see me like this. She said she loved me-- don't let her see me like--" Mathew said and lost consciousness.

Janet had to fasten her step backwards because once Mathew lost consciousness, his weight seemed to have doubled.

"His room is the first to the right," Mahon said, gave to Janet immediately the elevator opened, the keys which Janet reluctantly retrieved not believing how incompassionate Mahon really was. Janet walked out of the elevator, knowing that Mahon and the driver were behind her but she had the shock of her life because as soon as she stepped out, the elevator closed, Mahon and the driver inside, they had chosen to abandon her with the unconscious Mathew.

Janet stared at the elevator for a long time, she had left her phone in the black van in her strife to support Mathew out but she did not consider that now. She did not know what was wrong with Mathew and why he surrounded himself with people like Mahon, who never cared about him at all. She knew no one in Timmins except Rosemary who had just left for the U.S. she did not know her way around Timmins except for Moreal and the dinner Josh and Mike had taken her, she therefore didn't know where to start to seek medical help there in Timmins, it was clear that Mathew needed that and from how Stephen Mahon had behaved she doubted if Mathew got any of that. So after she would put him to sleep, she knew she would have to rush downstairs either to the reception or to his friends to seek for the help with Mathew as opposed to just standing there and staring at the elevator which had by now been closed for a minute.

She moved along with Mathew and at the room Mahon had told her, she turned the key and entered into a yet more spacious room, probably equal to her own but more bigger,it actually opened to several rooms and like hers it also had a nice view outside. She lowered Mathew on his couch and ran about to locate his bedroom. She opened one room and when she saw an equally exquisite room complete with a double sized bed, she ran to Mathew and helped him inside. She laid him on the bed. When she was about to go out of the room to seek help for Mathew something caught her interest. On the table next to Mathew's bed where a lot of magazines were, most of naked ladies, lay white powder, it looked as though it had been disturbed, like someone had run a hand on it and thus disturbed it.

She slowly approached the table, she knelt down, got some of the white powder by her hand and sniffed it. She immediately sneezed and she was sure it was an illegal drug. She stared away from the powder and looked over at Mathew, she couldn't believe he was into drugs, a realization which explained a lot and a lot about how he had behaved earlier when they were going to the concert. She then looked over at another desk where she saw a landline and a book beside it, she quickly rushed there, opened the book up, wishing that there could be atleast one number that she could call up in there and she did find Stephen Mahon's phone number. She frantically pressed the digits to call the man up so that he could see what was happening to the rock star but before she could press the call button, a sad realization overcame her, Stephen did know of Mathew's use of drugs, a reason which explained why he was hesitant about calling a physician for Mathew. Janet was saddened that Mahon allowed this behavior.

Confused, she walked out of Mathew's room and out of the penthouse, she left the keys by the couches in the living room and went out. She was tired and she just had the worst shock, now with conflicting thoughts about whether it would be alright for her to spend any more time with Mathew, she went to her room. At dinner time, she ate and when it was time to sleep she couldn't, a lot was on her mind for her to sleep. She instead stepped into the shower as she questioned what she had gotten herself into.

Now with the concert gone and her excitement about seeing Mathew in person gone, she actually began to question her further involvement with Mathew. He was a mess and she did not want to spend her life with a drug addict who could change moods anytime. And that was if her father would accept him. If things went any further, she knew her and him would never work out but she still loved him and she loved him so much that she firmly decided she was going to stand by him. She had found true love and she knew that no drug addiction would separate her from him. So she finished showering and late into the night, she closed her door and went back to his apartment instead. He needed care and she was willing to be by him. When she reached the penthouse, she found the door still not locked, when she entered, she was sure nobody had come inside after she had left the room. When she was inside, she went to the couches, got the keys and locked herself and Mathew inside, she then went to the bedroom and almost screamed from what she saw. Mathew had gotten up from his bed and was by the table. The white powder heap higher than when Janet had left it, his mouth and nose white from the powder and heaping more into himself.

"Stop!" Janet screamed.

"Janice?" Mathew said, looked sheepishly into her direction and tried to hide the powder away, he rubbed it off the table quickly that it sprayed across the floor.

"I have already seen it!"

"Are-- are you going to leave me? You had said you loved me," Mathew cried. Janet looked at Mathew confused at his behavior. She had thought that she was the one who was the desperate one there. Mathew was a rock star. Every girl's fantasy. But why did he cry for Janet to stay with him-- he had just met her yesterday and as opposed to her,Janet doubted Mathew loved her yet. Therefore she was certain he was still under the influence of drugs

"Come with me," Janet said and walked past Mathew, she was disappointed in Mathew but she didn't want it to show.

"Where are you taking me?" Mathew answered between sobs.

"Just come!" Janet said, Mathew got up and followed her, though reluctantly as if she was taking him to jail or as if he truly didn't want to go but had no choice but to do so.

Janet brought him to the bathroom, Mathew looked bewildered, she opened the door and motioned for him to get inside. Mathew hesitantly got in.

"I will refresh tomorrow," he complained but went inside. Janet was atleast glad that he understood her intentions. Once he was inside, Janet went and disconnected the geyser water and she only knew she had done a good job when Mathew screamed and tried to run away from the shower. But Janet pushed him inside, the cold water, she hoped, would do him good.

Mathew finished bathing, Janet waited for him by

the shower door and he came out of the bathroom with a headache. After he was nicely dressed, Janet took the liberty of requesting for some tea from room service. Then she searched for pain killers whilst Mathew lay on the bed, lustfully eyeing the white rubbed powder on the table but knew better off than to reach forward for it.

When he had taken his painkillers, drunk his tea, Mathew slept and Janet proceeded to clean his room and she discovered more white powder, many cigars, marijuana and in the cooler by his bed, assorted and fine wines and bottles of beer. Not only was Mathew a drug abuser he also abused alcohol and Janet didn't know the extent what all that had done to him or to his body and for how long he had been an addict.

And when she was done cleaning the room, she slept beside Mathew. And early the next morning Mathew was the first to get up and after a knock from the door and Mathew call out to answer the door did Janet wake up.

She opened her eyes and looked in the direction of Mathew and Mathew went away from view and after a few steps she heard him open the entrance door for the person who had been knocking. She then heard whispers.

"Scunka-- guys-- what are you doing here?" Mathew whispered.

"What sort of question is that?" Scunka replied.

"Yeah, we come here early in the morning to

check on your dead self and surprisingly today you are alive and had locked yourself in!"

"Quiet-- Janice is here."

"We see-- Good morning Janice!"

"I believe her name is Janet or have you Mathew also decided to give her another name?" Scunka said.

"I don't know what you are talking about-- rehearsals after an hour-- now please go."

"Not until we say hello to your 'new babe'," Martin said.

"Don't call her stupid names like those, she's a lady," Mathew said.

"Look who's saying that!" Scunka said.

"Please go away," Mathew now pleaded.

"Okay, but first. . . Good morning miss Mathew!"

"Good morning Scunka and everybody!" Janet exclaimed and smiled.

"Now look at what you've done. You've woken her--" Mathew said.

"Now we can get inside. Guys inside!"

"No!" Mathew said and Janet heard the door bang and then keys turn. She was sure Mathew had locked his friends outside the penthouse and she confined it when Mathew came to the bedroom alone.

"Did you hear me calling your name wrongly?"

Janet nodded.

"Sorry for that-- And huh, thank you for yesterday."

"What?" Janet asked. A lot had happened the

previous day that she didn't know what Mathew was thanking her for.

"I needed that bath, pretty badly."

"Oh that," Janet said and got off the bed. Mathew went to sit on the bed and Janet went for her shoes which were beside the bed.

"Come and sit with me."

Janet looked behind and she couldn't resist the pleading eyes of Mathew, so she went to him and on his bed right beside him she sat.

"I am guessing you know all about my addiction. So I beg of you to keep it a secret."

"You need to stop."

"I tried. I failed. There is no Mathew without what I do in here."

"You are destroying yourself."

"I gave up on thinking about that when I discovered this addiction is bigger than me and when I learned that it boosts my performance, I continued more freely with it and stopped pushing myself to stop."

"Tell me something?"

"What?" Mathew said. Janet looked him straight in the eyes.

"I want you to be honest with me--"

"Just ask me your question Janet."

"Where you high on drugs when you slept with me yesterday?"

"A little. I pumped up myself a lot more after that

before I could perform."

Janet was disappointed and she stood up. She couldn't believe that Mathew wasn't himself when he had sex with her the previous day. It pained her to realize that he couldn't have wanted her if he was normal and not on drugs. "Don't punish yourself. I know you don't like men who do drugs but I have confidence issues. After the pool, I spent the entire day locating your hotel room and after I had found it, I spent the next morning puffing on cigars and doing drugs to give me confidence to approach you, to tell you how beautiful you looked the previous day at the pool and to ask you out and whether it was true you loved me. I am sorry I took advantage of you. Everything happened so fast--"

"Yes for me too," Janet said and left the room.

"Give me a chance to prove myself. That I can also be a good man. That I can also love and be loved!" Mathew called out to Janet. Janet had by now reached the door of the penthouse and was turning the keys to open the door and get out of there. She knew that she loved Mathew but at that moment she realized that at the time when they had made out, she was the one in atleast a sound state of mind and it was her duty to stop the moment no matter how she loved and cherished it afterwards. "Don't leave me like this Janet," Mathew continued. Janet stopped. Mathew sobbed, his sobs louder to be ignored "Like you I am desperate. Like you I am desperate for love. You don't see it but we are meant for each other."

Janet went back to Mathew's bedroom.

"I am not desperate!" she lied and ran off.

"You are taking it the wrong way," Mathew said and ran after her, he overtook her and blocked the door. "I have finally found a good woman-- I saw how you took care of me yesterday-- and I ain't gonna let you go," Mathew said and leaned in to kiss Janet. Janet held his mouth in time and pushed him back.

"You are not going to have your way with me again-- what? Do you think this is a game?" Janet asked.

"Sorry," Mathew withdrew and concentrated on defending the door "I have never done this before-- I mean, be in love-- that was too fast, wasn't it-- I mean that I may learn to love you--"

"Are you moving or what?"

"What do you need me to do to make you understand?"

"I need you to move aside and let me pass. Clearly you are a mess. I never knew that the famous Mathew was this pathetic-- both normal and high on drugs."

"Alright, if you want to go--" Mathew said and stepped aside. "I don't know how to be romantic and I won't learn if you keep scolding me. Just like in high school, I was meant to be alone. I was a fool to dream otherwise. Please go miss Janet and thank you for your time," Mathew said. But Janet did not move and she stared at Mathew, sincerity pouring out of his eyes.

"Why aren't you leaving?"

"Because what you just did was romantic. I can see your honesty, your truth and I understand you now-- Is your being alone in high school the reason why you resorted to drugs?"

"Yes," Mathew said and walked inside the penthouse "I couldn't stand the loneliness. Nobody seemed to understand me that time and I seemed not to know how to make friends."

"I understand you and like you said we were destined to be together," Janet said whilst she walked inside the penthouse and followed Mathew to the couches where he flopped and tried to bury his face. "Destiny put me in your life, brought me from Saute Ste Marie to here and in this hotel so that I would love you and help you stop a habit which has lavished you for years," Janet said, she was now beside Mathew on the couch. She lifted his chin and stared deep into his eyes.

"I am sure you will leave me when you discover that is impossible. Nobody has ever been able to help me quit the habit that I gave up trying," Mathew said sincerely.

"That is because nobody has loved you like I do. Believe me when you let love lead, that habit is no match. Let me love you and my heart is open to your love. Let us fight through this addiction together. We are stronger than it. When we stand together and love each other, I am sure we may overcome even the impossible," Janet said and moved closer to Mathew.

Mathew as if afraid of what was about to happen trembled, tied his lips together and closed his eyes. Janet brought her face closer to Mathew's, her lips closer to his, Mathew breathed heavily, Janet slowly parted Mathew's lips and she could feel that Mathew was expecting her touch. His lips were supple and when she finally kissed him, Mathew responded with just as much intensity and passion as what Janet kissed him with. Mathew was compassionate and a lover and from how rampantly their hearts bet together when they kissed each other on that couch, Janet could see that Mathew was a better lover when sober than when on drugs and she decided to help him quit drugs. She loved him and she needed a sober Mathew to love her too.

Chapter Four

Janet lived another two days in the hotel room Josh had booked her and in those two days she did not forget about Josh, his guitar was sited at the corner in her room next to Mathew's, she after all had not seen a man as persistent as Josh and she did not want to give up on his friendship no matter how twisted a turn their new relationship had taken. So in those two days she tried to look for him but with no phone on her, all she could end up was by his office which had remained closed and locked since the last time she saw him and also by the gates, by the two guards who also were worried for Josh, they also had not seen him since that time he stormed off and didn't say anything to them.

At the end of the two days, Janet gave up on Josh and actually concentrated on her wonderful, new found relationship. Mathew was adorable, charming and recovering. He had not done any drugs for two days now and Janet appreciated his efforts even though at times he would shiver as his eyes darted about the room looking for any stash but with the drugs thrown out and Janet strictly warning Stephen Mahon not to encourage him or buy drugs for him any longer-- she had discovered that his manager not only encouraged the vice but enhanced it also-- Mathew would recuperate after talking to her. She would take care of him, help him calm down during his refractory stages, have a cold bath ready for him, get him coffee, pain killers, tea or anything which would have a soothing effect on him and he would calm down and sleep off his addiction.

Mathew's friends were surprised when she told them that Mathew had been doing drugs but the way they exclaimed their "you don't mean it," "No way!" was suspicious and Janet knew that they had known all the time. They however were supportive of his recovery even more than his addiction because unlike what she had last seen when she came to the penthouse, his friends now visited him more often and stayed around a little longer.

In those two days she had grown to love Mathew more. Apart from all that glamour and excitement about his being a superstar, a rock star, Janet found that Mathew was an ordinary boy. He talked like one, laughed like one, and kissed like one, and that aspect intoxicated her that she couldn't think of anyone else other than him. Nobody could love her better than Mathew did and she was not wrong in giving their relationship a chance. And no matter how desperate she had appeared at first there at the swimming pool, when she saw how he smiled when she smiled at him and how he couldn't stand it when she went back to her room, Janet knew that moment was worth it. She cherished it and so did Mathew.

After the two days, when she was scheduled to leave the hotel, early in the morning she heard a knock on her door and knowing that it would be Mathew, he had developed a habit of waking her up like that in the morning, she jumped up out of the bed and went to the door and she had been right, it was Mathew. He looked jubilant, his face radiated with happiness, his smile went sideways to all sides of his face.

"What?" Janet asked, she smiled, Mathew's happiness was contagious.

"You look beautiful today."

"And you look handsome my rock star," Janet said, Mathew stared down. Janet expectant of what Mathew would say next and she knew Mathew had a habit of looking down for a long time when he was complimented. With his smile still fixed and his eyes darting expectedly, he looked back at her after a few seconds. Janet stood looking at him.

"I want to take you out. Not around the hotel but-
-"

"Surprise me," Janet said and pulled him inside and hugged him very tightly "Good morning." Mathew kissed her on the forehead and she released him. "Wait for me to get ready better yet, come with me to the bathroom. There, you will tell me stories whilst I bath and look beautiful especially for you my darling."

"I have a better proposal--"

"but it will involve you sitting by the bathroom door, right?"

"Whatever you say my Janet-- here's what I was thinking. You have my guitar and I am a rock star--"

"Yes--" Janet couldn't contain her excitement.

"I will sing that slow love song I usually perform alone whilst you take a bath."

"You mean that song you sang at the wedding?"

"What wedding?"

"The one you did here?"

"Oh, that one-- and speaking of that wedding. The fellow who booked my services, Josh, payed my manager pretty well. I was surprised at the amount of money I received from that one show and a single song-- by the way that day I tried to visit his office, found it locked and the man walking away from it very furiously. I called out to him, he looked at me, angry than before and sped off. I tried running after him but after I got to the parking lot, I already found him leaving in his car. He nearly ran over me. What he saw must have pissed him off."

"Because he did not know what kind of guy you were. He was only concerned for me. He is a good friend and I am sure that when he learns that you love me like I do love you, he will be glad we are together."

When Janet was ready and well dressed for

Mathew's surprise, right after she had taken a bath with Mathew singing her on, and after she had confirmed that Mathew was thoughtful to promise lunch and breakfast to wherever they were going, Janet made it out of her room and with her rubbing shoulders with Mathew whilst he carried the guitar he got from Janet's room, they went down and into the parking lot of the hotel. And when Janet saw that Mathew was going towards the creepy black van she had to stop him. "There is no way I am going into that car!" she said and Mathew had to book another car. A good looking one with no roof on top and with transparent glasses and they got in and left the hotel.

Janet expected that Mathew would take her somewhere crowded, to some diner or restaurant but when he pulled off before a cliff, she abandoned all her expectations.

They were now in a forest, trees darted to the left side and over after a cliff down below looked deadly, a pit which was dangerous even when looking down it. It was green there and small insects clicked about whilst Mathew and Janet stood on the cliff, their booked car just a few inches from it and behind them.

After inspecting down, Janet walked backwards but Mathew kept walking forward until he could not move any farther without falling down the cliff.

"Why have you brought me here?" Janet asked. But Mathew kept quiet. He spread his arms open wide and closed his eyes and smiled. "It is not funny, you will fall. One step forward--" but Mathew drew his finger to his mouth to silence Janet. He turned and walked to Janet. He held out both his hands and called out to her.

"Come. I wanted to show you this."

Janet trusted him with all her heart and went to him. Together they walked to the cliff as they held each other's hands, Janet wondering what was so special about that cliff and why Mathew beamed when he looked down it. She continued to wonder whilst Mathew once again held his eyes closed and smiled letting the air come rushing past him.

"I have finally found love mother. Dad. Her name is Janet, I am here to introduce her to you. I am sure you approve of her wherever you are," Mathew said. Janet became confused. Mathew never talked about his parents and when he had said it, it was on top of a cliff, something was amiss, and she needed to find out what it was.

"What is happening Mathew?" Janet asked. Mathew opened his eyes, stared at Janet and smiled at her even more. It was like he was relieved. Like a heavy burden had been taken off him and he, still holding Janet's hand walked back with her to the car and on the car front, they both sat, Janet expectant of what Mathew had to say. She kept quiet and let Mathew talk.

"My parents died here," Mathew said.

"I am sorry," Janet said. Mathew scoffed.

"You should have seen me before you came into

my life. Then you would have truly felt sorry for me-- I would come here and weep for them instead of smiling."

"You think that I am not sorry?"

"I am not saying that. I know you are--" Mathew said and caressed Janet's hand "Come," he said and Janet shifted from her sit and now sat on Mathew's lap. "All I am saying is that before you came, I used to cry a lot. I had to advocate for my manager to put three shows for me in Timmins just for me to be here a little longer and come and visit this cliff. I began drugging myself ever since my parents died when I was 15, I couldn't coup with their loss and the loneliness at school only intensified my--"

"You should have told me about your parents earlier."

"I am doing that now--"

"I would have known how to go about therapy for your addiction if I knew about your loss."

"You are all the therapy I need, see, I am doing better now with you on my side."

"I think you need professional help. There is a good rehabilitation center in Toronto--"

"No, I am not going there. I think I am improving with your help alone and so do my friends."

"But--"

"Your love is all I need," Mathew said and Janet kept quiet knowing well that she could not convince Mathew otherwise. She atleast had her questions when she came to Timmins answered. She now knew why Mathew had decided to do three shows-- which were later reduced to two-- in Timmins alone. And after some silence, Mathew caressing Janet's hand in front whilst he hugged her from the back, he continued, "My parents were here to celebrate their 17th wedding anniversary. They had just renewed their wedding vows at Crystal hotel and after a week's stay there, they were leaving for America when my father lost control of his car and the car wandered off road and drove straight for the cliff--"

"Is that the reason why you performed at Rosemary's wedding. You were doing it for your parents?"

"Yes. I had agreed to do it for free. But I later found out that my manager had gone behind my back and ripped Josh of all the money he could get for my act that night. I have never performed for weddings you know but I did it for my parents and after I saw how happy the couple were, I guessed that must have been how happy my parents were after they retook their vows, I was in school back then, but I knew they were that happy also-- but as you will guess after the performance I felt pain and blamed myself for their deaths and went straight from there to my room to do drugs."

"Why do you blame yourself? It is not your fault that they died. You couldn't have done anything even if you wanted to."

"That is where you are wrong-- If I went with them on their trip instead of concentrating on a science project I was to submit in school that fall, maybe I could have saved them. I shouldn't have stayed back and valued a thing I later didn't even complete."

"You didn't finish your science project?"

"Not only that, I later quit school altogether after a year at it after my parent's death and seeing that it did not feel right any more. I was devastated and kept at drugs until Mr Mahon discovered the talent in me and still encouraging me to do drugs, I learnt on how to channel my frustrations and disappointments in life to music but now I have you-- because of you I have learnt to love, no one came close to me before you. I was this lonely drug addict and I in time learnt to live alone and kept at this even when I became successful in music, with you I know the power of love. Never would I have imagined I would go one hour without doing drugs or smoking or drinking but look at me now, three days straight and I am one hundred percent sober. Never would I come here and smile but look at me now--"

"Shh," Janet put a finger on Mathew's lips and pulled him from the car. She was now the one who dragged him to the cliff and when they stood, she let herself be hugged by Mathew from the back, she reasoned that he must have been wondering what she was up to. She held his hands very tightly and shouted ahead "I love your son very much and for as long as I am with him I promise that I will make him see that it was not his fault you are not with him now and I also promise that I will help him the best I can and that I will love him unconditionally. I however require your blessings for me to do that. Bless us. Bless this wonderful love we share--"

"Thank you, and I am sure they have blessed us and blessed our love," Mathew whispered to Janet.

"Where did you bury your parents?" Janet asked.

"In North Hampshire, my home state. Why?"

"I would also like to visit their graves."

"Sure."

Janet stood in that position for some time, neither her nor Mathew saying a thing. She couldn't believe that there was so much pain in Mathew's life but she knew that she was there in his life for a reason and she meant it when she had asked for his parent's blessings. Mathew rested on her and he appeared so calm and so composed that Janet was glad that he valued her as much as she valued him. He loved her. He had just told his parents so. Janet couldn't have been more happier that she got to share Mathew's painful memories as she did his happy ones.

"We have to go back," Janet finally said and turned back to walk towards the car, she dragged Mathew along and he silently obeyed. "You know that I have to move out of my hotel room today, right?"

"Yes I do and I am sure by the time we get back there, Scunka and the boys would have finished moving your things into my penthouse--"

"You want me to move in with you?" Janet asked, excitement escaping through her voice.

"Yes. You know I can not live without you and therefore that means our trip to Saute Ste Marie will have to wait."

"You want to come to Saute Ste Marie too?"

"Did you think I would let you go back alone?" Mathew said. Janet couldn't contain her happiness any longer. She jumped onto Mathew, he lost his balance and fell down and on top of him she lay, kissing him all over.

"You don't know how happy you make me," Janet said and kissed him again.

"No, I am the happiest one here," Mathew teasingly replied and kissed her back. They played like this rolling on the ground whilst they kissed. They stared at each other in the eyes, they both couldn't give that moment for anything until Mathew started to get up and say something about them not having ate anything since the hotel. He then went to the car, leaving Janet lying down there and starring upwards, and he got the lunch he had parked for both of them.

"We came here on empty stomachs and we will not go back as we came," he said and served them both the food. They sat to eat, they sat on the cliff, they talked, they laughed and also had lunch there and by the time they realized that they had planned on getting back for Mathew's rehearsal, it was already late and the sun was already setting.

"Time does fly when you are in love, doesn't it?" Mathew said and got up. He pulled Janet up and she laughed. She tried to pick up the disposable drink cans but Mathew refused her and pulled her to the car. She giggled as Mathew attempted to be romantic by opening the door for her.

"You are such a gentleman," she teased and entered into the car. Mathew entered and with the guitar still at the back of the vehicle, they went off and sped through the early night to the hotel and to Mathew's penthouse.

At Mathew's penthouse she stayed up late, whilst Mathew slept soundly, she silently waited for her period but it never came. It seemed strange to her but she always was spot on when counting her period days and she knew she must have it that time. However when she disregarded her apprehension, maybe it would be the next day, she went to sleep beside Mathew.

Early the next morning, they were disturbed with the familiar knock and without hesitation, Janet got up, she knew who it was who was at the door. She went there, leaving Mathew as he went to the bathroom to freshen up before he could be fully awake. She opened the door and found Scunka, Martin, Gerald and Mr Mahon by the door.

"Do you like your new room?" Mr Stephen Mahon asked.

"Yes-- Please come in," Janet said.

"Don't try to decorate this place. We will be leaving Canada in the next three days," Scunka said.

"I know that and I promise I won't, thank you for helping me with my things."

"Don't mention it," Mr Mahon said.

"You also went to my room?"

"Yes unfortunately. Tried to refuse but sober Mathew said I got paid to do that--"

"I did not tell you that!" Mathew shouted from the bathroom.

"And what I saw in there will haunt me for the rest of my life," Mr Mahon continued as if he hadn't been disturbed.

"Come on Mahon, it was just some underwear and some bikinis nothing horrifying about that," Scunka said. Janet regretted having allowed Mathew to talk her into staying at the cliff whilst his friends did her packing.

"Still. I have never seen anything like those before," Mr Mahon said and smiled at Janet.

"Grow up Mr Mahon and you three, you should have let the female attendants of the hotel do the packing," Janet said. Mathew came out of the bathroom, with a towel rapped around him, running.

"Who among you four touched my fiancee's underwear?"

"Relax dude, none of us. Mr Mahon is just joking. None of us even did the packing, we just supervised it--now will you go back to the shower?" martin said and all four of them laughed. Mathew went back.

"All of you please relax. Sit down and tell me what I would offer you."

"Whisky-- Brandy-- two touts of spirit for me," they said.

"You know I threw those away. Drinks? Any of you want drinks?"

"Never," they refused.

"Then enjoy watching television whilst you wait for him. And if any of you like I would offer you water," Janet said and at this they all laughed as if she was crazy saying what she had just said.and then Mathew came back. Janet left them and went to the bedroom, she needed to wash up, and change.

"Are you sure you don't have any whisky?" Janet heard one of Mathew's friends say.

"No," Mathew quickly replied.

"What has she done to you, dude?" another asked.

"I can hear that!" Janet called out from the shower.

"I am a changed man guys," Mathew told his friends who scoffed.

"We shall see about that. I can't believe a man can change so suddenly so soon."

"I still can hear you. You are supposed to be encouraging him not laughing at him."

"Yes mum, we are sorry mum," Martin said and all three of Mathew's friends laughed.

"So funny," Janet said and continued to shower.

When she had finished showering and dressed up,

she went to the room where Mathew and his friends were and after a couple of minutes they got up to leave. Mathew sat with Janet, he did not even offer to see them to the door.

“I hope you will not miss rehearsals today. Mr Mahon told us that we need to record something whilst we are here. Don’t miss it and you miss Mathew, make sure he comes today,” martin said, pointing at Janet.

“Alright, he will come. In fact he will go with you now. I don’t need him,” Janet said.

“Oh. . . Looks like she’s grown tired of you dude,” Scunka said. Mathew protested but reluctantly got up and went after his friends.

“I need you Mr Mahon to remain with me. I need to talk to you,” Janet said. Mr Mahon looked stunned and turned back.

Mathew’s friends laughed. “And she already found a replacement for you. Old Mahon,” Scunka said and then the two of his friends laughed.

“Don’t joke like that,” Mathew said. Martin opened the door and Mathew passed through the door first and Scunka and Gerald followed along.

“You could do with a bottle of whisky now,” Martin said, and closed the door.

:”Janet told me not to--”

“She’s with the old man now--”

“Martin, don’t you dare. I thought you were supporting your friend!”

“Yes mum, just testing his resistance and it is

strong!" Martin called out and afterwards the four voices were within no earshot to be heard.

Janet then returned her attention to Stephen Mahon who was still standing beside the door, stunned that Janet had called him.

"Please sit," Janet said. Stephen slowly approached the couches and sat down. He starred at Janet inquisitively as if he was trying to study her. "I know we never got to agree on most things and when I discovered that you were supporting Mathew's drug addiction I told you off, therefore I know I may not be your favorite person here--"

"That is because we got off to the wrong start. I was untrusting when I first met you but later I knew you meant well for Mathew--"

"Just let me finish--"

"Okay, go on."

"I need your help."

"If it is concerning Mathew I am willing to help."

"Good then." Janet stood up "Drink?" Mr Mahon laughed and nodded.

"Anything. You may even bring me water," he said and continued to laugh.

Janet served both of them a drink. She poured in two glasses a green drink which Stephen Mahon was glad to gush down and she poured another. Clearly he was nervous.

"You may guess that you weren't my favorite person either especially when you left me with a sick and unconscious Mathew standing just outside the elevator. He had not been well and you didn't care."

"Because I knew what was wrong with him."

"Anyway I am glad that you are supporting his recovery and I need you to support him even further-- I may never know why you supported and bought drugs for him but I need you to see to it that he receives none especially when he goes back home."

"You are not coming with him?"

"I will join him if he asks me to. But you and I know that will not be anytime sooner. If he does ask me to come, I will have to get a passport, process a visa and such documentation takes days."

"Don't worry then, he is in good hands. And if I may defend myself, I bought drugs for him because I did not know what to do with him. He had already started the addiction on himself, there was no way that I could have stopped it and I am glad that you are trying and he is recuperating--"

"There is no forgiving what you did," Janet said. Mr Mahon suddenly nodded.

"You are good company for him and all his friends are saying so. Whatever you are doing, keep at it--"

"I am afraid it may not be enough-- I underestimated the emotional extent of his addiction but now I fully understand it and that is why I want you to promise me that you will get him rehabilitated when you take him back. He needs professional help--"

"But the music?"

"His heath is more important," Janet said. Mr Mahon seemed to hesitate. "Please tell me we are on the same page here--"

"He loves what he does. I am not sure he will accept being out of action--"

"I will convince him to. Besides it will just be maybe up to six months and after that he will do all the music he wants," Janet said. Mr Mahon seemed to consider what Janet said and after a while he agreed with her.

"Do what you have to. I will support you and I promise that I will do everything you have asked me for Mathew. I owe him that after encouraging his vice," he said and Janet bid goodbye to him.

In the next two days, she kept watch on her period but it never came. And late at night, she finally gathered up the courage to go down from the penthouse to check if her suspicions were correct. She had by now gotten used to the hotel that she knew her way around the place. She went down, got herself a pregnancy tester and in the bathroom of the penthouse she did the pregnancy test and confirmed what she had suspected. She was pregnant. She was happy but she did not know if Mathew would marvel at the news and she definitely knew that her parents wouldn't be pleased when they learnt of her pregnancy. She could almost feel her father's disappointment and her mother's scolding her about getting pregnant outside wedlock.

She went back to sleep, she did not dare wake Mathew about the news because she did not know how he could react when he heard the news.

Early the next day they were supposed to move out and everything had been packed. Mathew woke up early and went away. Janet wondered where he could have gone to so early but she finally settled for the idea that he had gone to visit his friends in their rooms for a change before they all finally moved out.

Mathew had promised Janet that he would personally take her home, and Janet knew that he couldn't go back on his word. And so without worrying much about where Mathew had gone too, she got up, cleaned up, got dressed, ate her breakfast and carried outside the penthouse a suitcase which was now three times bigger than the one she had come with to Timmins.

She left the penthouse door open and went straight for the elevator and when she was down, she carried her suitcase along to the parking lot and straight to the black glass tinted van that she despised so much. She had last got on that car when Mathew had taken her to a concert and even though she felt tense about getting on it, she knew she had to. After all that was the car Mathew traveled in to conceal his identity from people in the streets. But when she got to the car, there was no one there.

She had hoped to find all the men down there but now that they weren't down, she thought about going back into the hotel and searching for them. She couldn't wait all day down there. But when that thought beamed in her mind did a car drive into the packing lot. It caught her attention because it was heading straight for her. She recognized the car, it was the one that Mathew had booked and taken her in to the cliff. And Mathew was at the driver's seat driving the vehicle. She was glad that Mathew had considered how she hated to drive in the black van and had booked that car again.

Mathew inside the car grinned and so was Mr Mahon, Gerald, Scunka, and Martin-- they all smiled at her before they got out of the vehicle.

"Hello beautiful, waited long?" Mathew asked.

"Almost went up," Janet replied "--and I couldn't have found you there," she said.

"Yes because we went and--" Mr Mahon started but was interrupted by Mathew.

"Dude. What is wrong with you? Respect. But I thought that I was the one who would tell her," Mathew said. Stephen Mahon surrendered.

Mathew leaned closer to Janet. Janet wondered what was wrong. Mathew smiled and was about to speak before Scunka broke in.

"We bought you this vehicle," he said. Mathew was furious.

"Scunka you are out of my band," Mathew said.

"As if you can do without me," Scunka said and laughed.

"Is it true Mathew?" Janet asked.

"Yes it is. But I did. Not we--" Mathew said and looked at his friends. They kept quiet.

"Of course you did. And thank you, how thoughtful but you didn't have to buy me the car, you could have rented it like the last time after all Saute Ste Marie is in Canada. The company could have picked it up--"

"Are you kidding?-- We have moments in this car, I just thought that--"

"Speak no more, I understand. We visited the cliff together in this car, how could I ever forget that," Janet said and went to Mathew. She kissed him and he kissed her back, they would have continued if not for Janet who realized that Mathew's friends and manager were right there watching.

"Why did you stop?" Scunka asked "I was loving the show."

"Scunka stop it. I will throw you out of the band if you continue," Mathew shyly said.

"Look at him he's shy," Martin joined in.

"You too Martin," Mathew said.

"And then what band will you have?" Scunka said and they laughed. "One of these days if these threats continue, we may consider throwing you out of the band ourselves."

"What?-- You can't do that, I am Mathew, remember?"

"Stop it all three of you-- Mathew do what you

came here to do so that we may all leave," Stephen Mahon said.

"Thank you man. That is why I hired you, you are always useful not Scunka and martin, always commenting on anything. Anymore time with them, I may never marry."

"Just get on with it-- and for the record, all of you here, I discovered Mathew, he did not hire me."

"Same thing man," Mathew shrugged and was on his knees in front of Janet. Janet wondered what he was up to but she did not have to wait long enough because after seconds when he had knelt, he released a ring from his pocket. Janet held her face with her hands, she knew what Mathew was going to do. She had not expected it and tears began to form in her eyes.

"My lovely Janet. My love. My one and only-- the one who rocks my life--" Mathew held the ring but he was interrupted by his friends.

"Come on. You are overdoing it--" Scunka said. Mathew looked sharply at him and instantly Scunka kept quiet. He returned his gaze to Janet and proceeded to smile as before as if he had not been disturbed.

"Will you marry me?" Mathew asked. Janet cried and nodded her head, she could not believe it. The man she loved had just asked her to marry her. She had to be dreaming, so she screamed.

"Yes!-- Yes I will Mathew!" Janet said and Mathew's friends and the manager broke in applause. They were sitting by the car. Gerald the quiet one at the front but when she had agreed he was the loudest and whistled so much that Janet's ears hurt.

Mathew got up and with Janet still sobbing from the excitement, he held her close and put the ring on the finger whose hand Janet had extended and the two kissed. Unlike earlier, Janet did not mind who was watching, she kept kissing Mathew and pretended nothing other than Mathew existed and in her mind, nothing did other than her love. She was happy and so was Mathew.

"I am so happy. I had thought you would say no."

"Why would I-- You know I love you," Janet said.

"And I love you too," Mathew said and the man behind broke into more applause. They now started to come down the car, probably to congratulate the couple when Janet whispered to Mathew amidst their passionate kiss.

"I have news that will make you more happy-- I am pregnant. You are going to be a father," Janet whispered. Mathew let go of her and turned to his friends.

"Yes!" he exclaimed. His friends became quiet. They knew Mathew was happy but they couldn't understand the sudden change of behavior. He ran to Gerald first, then to Martin, to Scunka and finally to Mr Mahon "I am going to be a father guys, me a father!" he said, clearly he was excited and Janet was happy that he was. Atleast he would share that joy with him.

"Geeze man, congratulations," Gerald said. Mr

Mahon hugged him tightly.

"What joy-- another rock star. You know what this means right?-- We will make a lot of money from baby products advertisements. We may also advocate for a clothing line to be opened under his name. Who wouldn't want products with you and your baby's name tied to them--"

"Not now Mahon. Hold it, the baby is barely days old and you are busy thinking about money. Shame on you man!" Scunka said. But before he could continue, Mathew went to Scunka and hugged him tightly also that Scunka appeared as though he was grasping for air "I will be an uncle!" he managed to say.

But Mr Mahon wasn't done because he came to Janet who was crying with joy seeing how ecstatic Mathew was when he heard the news. "Don't be like your soon-to-be husband and his friend Scunka. No wonder he was named that. You are the baby's mother. You know what opportunities lie ahead, don't you? Here I will explain--"

"Can't this conversation wait until the baby is born?" Janet asked.

"Right. I was just too excited. By the way congratulations on your pending marriage and on the upcoming superstar," Mr Mahon said.

"Thank you," Janet replied and proceeded to shake Mr Mahon's hand. She then proceeded to be congratulated by all of Mathew's friends, even Gerald, the silent one was overexcited.

When all his friends had congratulated her, Mathew came towards her, he was now crying when he went over and held her hands.

"What did I ever do to deserve such a good woman?" he asked. Janet didn't know how to answer his question. "And now you give me a son. I wish my parents could have been here to see this day," he said and cried out loud. His friends including the manager left them, clearly they had seen those two needed their privacy.

Mr Mahon came to them when Martin, Gerald, and Scunka had gone to the black van.

"Take your time. I am sure you know the way Mathew?" Stephen Mahon asked. Mathew still crying nodded.

"I can't trust you on that. Janet be sure to show him the way to Saute Ste Marie--"

"You are going there?"

"Yes, we promised Mathew that we would escort him to your house. And help him ask for your hand in marriage from your parents. He is afraid of your father--"

"The plans have changed," Mathew said.

"You no longer desire to go to Saute Ste Marie?" Mahon asked.

"No not that-- Now that I am going to be a father, I want to be rehabilitated fast for my child and that means I am willing to go to that rehabilitation center you mentioned Janet-- "

"Really?" Janet asked, Mathew answered, "Yes."

"It better be for only six months as you promised Janet. We will keep Mathew's fans preoccupied with his wedding news until he comes back from rehabilitation. We already have three songs we did here. I am sure that will keep things in check until he comes back."

"Yes Mr Mahon. I am sure it will be even less than six months."

"Good then, I have to tell the boys-- but for all this to work you need to get married soon and before rehabilitation."

"Yes Stephen, we will get married during this week if Janet's father agrees."

"Me and the boys will make sure he does," Mahon broke in.

"And after we are married we will stay back in Saute Ste Marie for some time before we leave for Toronto."

"As long as it will be in less than six months, I will be okay with it."

"And when I come back. I am coming back a brand new person. With my wife--" Mathew said and held Janet's nose and continued to cry. Janet smiled. "And the beautiful baby inside her. Together we shall rock the world again," he said and sobbed into Janet's hands.

"Alright son, hurry up," Mr Mahon said, parted Mathew on the back and went to the van. Seconds late, the van erupted in noise and it left the parking lot leaving the couple standing in the parking lot still holding hands.

Minutes passed. The couple kept starring at each other and finally Mathew said something. "I am speechless. You don't know what joy you have given me today," he said.

"If we continue like this we may not go from here, remember the cliff," Janet said. Mathew chuckled, he obviously remembered that they had stayed late, talking on the cliff.

"You are right-- We have an hour from Saute Ste Marie and the rest of our lives to talk. Let us go to tough man to ask for your hand in marriage," he said, released his hands from hers and reached for the suitcase which sat beside Janet where she had stood.

"I am excited," Janet said and wiped the tears from her face.

"Not as much as me," Janet replied and put the suitcase in the car. Mathew wiped his tears. "May we leave now?" Mathew said and opened the car door for Janet. He went around the car when she had got in and before he could get in, he asked her another question, "Have you got everything that belongs to you from the penthouse?"

"Yes. I left the door open though. In case you wanted to get something from there."

"Everything of mine is in the van. Scunka packed it and they went with it. Lets go then," Mathew said and sat in the car.

"Be a gentleman and go ahead and lock the door. Submit the keys and then we will go," Janet said. Mathew protested but he finally stepped out and ran out of the parking lot. Janet waited and she waited for a long time.

Thirty minutes in the car, she finally found Mathew's not coming back from the penthouse strange. She opened her door and went out to look for him. Each time swearing that if he had wanted to prank her into worrying for him, she would surely scold him and tell him that whatever his antics were, they were not funny.

She went into the hotel, asked by the reception if Mathew had left the keys by there and when the receptionist didn't confirm it, she went into the elevator and up the elevator to the floor containing the penthouse.

When the elevator stopped, She went out of the elevator and went inside the penthouse through the door which was now wide open. Clearly Mathew had entered there and she was sure he was still there, probably hiding, wanting her to come look for him. Such behavior was unusual of him, but under such circumstances she could not think of anything else which could have explained Mathew's delay in going back to the car in the parking lot.

"Mathew we are late. What is keeping you!?" Janet called out whilst she entered through the door but what she found just a few meters from the door had her terrified.

On the floor was blood, which had been rubbed against as if someone had dragged something on it. She held her chest as it beat, she followed the rubbed blood. Her heart beat fast in her chest. She did not know what to make of what she had just seen and therefore she just followed it inside. She walked slowly as she kept her gaze down.

"Mathew?" she called out now in a whisper and continued to follow the blood trail to Mathew's bedroom.

She heard someone move in the bedroom, and she ran inside. "Mathew what happened in here?" she asked as she emerged in the bedroom. But it was not Mathew who was in the bedroom but another man. Mathew's body lay on the floor beside the bed, the man had been trying to drag it when she had entered. Janet didn't know if she was to feel the terror because of Mathew's body which lay on the floor or surprise at the man who stood beside the body holding a gun but she did feel both and ran over to Mathew and at his side she fell down. The man holding the gun looking down on her.

"What are you doing here. I thought that you must be in Saute Ste Marie by now," the man said.

But Janet couldn't pay attention to him, she turned Mathew aside and saw that he had been shot in the chest. She tried to relive him but it was clear that the rock star, her love was no more, yet she tried.

"Wake up Mathew. Please don't leave me alone," Janet said and held his head. She tried to open his eyes but the life-less eyes didn't give her any hope. Tried resuscitation but she knew she had been late. He was already dead.

"I have killed him. He was the only one who was between our love and now with him gone we may pick up from where we left off," the man said. Janet looked up at him, tears rolling from her eyes at the realization of what he had done.

"What have you done Josh. How could you kill the man I love?" Janet asked, sobbing uncontrollably whilst she held Mathew's head in her laps. Josh came close to her, he pulled her off Mathew and made her stand but the strength in Janet had given out. The shock she felt seemed to have supped the strength from her legs and she could not stand. She fell right back to Mathew's body.

"You don't love him. You love me. It's me Josh. You told me not to give up on you and I just did that. I was going to come to Saute Ste Marie after here to ask for your hand in marriage. I thought you had gone back, what are you still doing here--"

"Shut up Josh. What made you think I loved you?" Janet screamed at Josh who looked pale and skinny than the last time she had seen him.

"But-- you--"

"I lied to you to be with Mathew. This is the man I love. I always have--"

"You used me--"

"Yes. Yes I did. But now that you know, help me. Help me get medical attention for him. He may be alive," Janet said, stood up and held Josh by the collars of his dirty tuxedo. It was clear he had not had a bath for days.

"He is dead and I am glad I killed him," Josh said and pushed Janet down. She fell down but as soon as she touched the ground, she looked up at Josh and got up again.

"You bastard. How could you. You monster," Janet cried and bet her punches frantically on Josh who stood his ground with his gun still in hand "We have a baby coming. We could have been a beautiful family. What did I ever do to you for you to destroy my happiness like this?" She continued to cry and beat Josh. Josh then tightly held her hand and brought her closer to him. He grew more angry. Janet stopped crying in anticipation of what Josh was going to do to her.

"What baby?" he asked. Janet kept silent obviously what she had said had angered him even more. "I am asking you a question Janet. You allowed yourself to be impregnated by him. Tell me when this happened-- was it that time when you allowed him to sleep with you in the hotel room that I booked for you," he said and pushed Janet. She stumbled on Mathew's body but she kept her balance. "How could you be so inhuman Janet. How could you allow him on you and right in my eyes!?

I wanted to convince myself that he had just taken advantage but you enjoyed it, didn't you, whore?"

"Josh let go of me," Janet desperately said as she tried to get Josh to let go of her hand.

"What is this. You also agreed to marry him. What had you told me when I proposed-- All in due time. But you meet this good for nothing musician sleep with him the second day and when he proposes marriage you agree instantly. I guess you must have been laughing at me when you two made out. And about what fool Josh is. What I did wrong was to love you. To sincerely love you. Did I commit a crime in doing that? Tell me!" Josh said.

Janet struggled to get herself out of his grip.

"Why did you give me false hope?"

"I am sorry Josh. I wanted to apologize but your office was locked since that day--"

"Quiet! Yes, since that day you made a mockery of my love for you, isn't that what you wanted to say?"

"No--"

"You love your boyfriend so much, don't you?" Josh said. Janet kept quiet and stared at the man who had once been lovable and charming and he was now a mess. He looked like one and acted like one and at that moment she too feared for her life. "Then you will die with him!" he said, released her and she had a second to realize what he had meant because as soon as he released her, she ran for her life. She didn't want to die with a symbol of her and Mathew's love still inside her.

She wanted to live for her and Mathew's child and she wasted no time than to ran for the door.

Josh probably realized what she was doing and he ran after her. She rushed through the penthouse entrance door and forward to the elevator. She pressed the button, and the elevator opened. Somehow, Josh had remained inside. She was glad and she immediately stepped inside the elevator and when the elevator doors were closing, Josh came form the penthouse at full speed running towards the elevator, vengeance evident in his eyes.

And in time the elevator closed. Janet heard Josh take the stairs. It was a race for her and her baby's life and Janet prayed that the elevator reached the reception before Josh did. And it did. Janet got out of the elevator and when she heard running footsteps getting closer she wasted no time than to run to the parking lot. She ran into the parking lot and got into the car that Mathew had bought for her, with her suitcase at the back, she started the ignition and reversed the car. On her back mirror she saw Josh emerge from the hotel and start to run after her, his firearm drawn at her. She ducked and continued driving backwards and as soon as she had space to, she drove out of the parking lot at full speed. Josh stared at her go before he too, went inside the parking lot, Janet knew he was to get his car. He was that determined to kill her and Janet knew it. So she wasted no time that when she was nearing the gate she screamed at Jod, the gateman to open the gate and before it was even half open she passed through it and rushed away.

She knew where Josh would go first and she avoided the road leading there. If her and her baby were to be safe, Janet knew that she had to avoid going back to Saute Ste Marie. On the next road, she turned and sped along hoping that Josh had taken the opposite road instead. Mathew had told her that his parents had died by the cliff when they were going back home, so she reasoned that the road at the cliff led to America. She had never been out of Canada before but she knew that her and her child's chances of survival were there in Ameriaca and not in Canada. Apart from Saute Ste Marie, she only knew of Moreal motel and Crystal hotel in Timmins and nowhere else and unfortunately Josh knew those places too. There was no way she would hide from him in Canada and she doubted if she was going to hide away from him for much longer where she planned on going either. He had the same address as hers to Mike and Rosemary's apartment in Florida and it couldn't be long before he went there to check if she had gone there when he exhausted his options of searching for her. Janet only hoped that that would be at least after nine months. Because after that, she would have given birth to Mathew's child and gone to look for Mathew's family to explain to them whom she was and what had happened to Mathew.

She sped along the road by the cliff. She would take her chances with the customs officers by the border than with Josh. She looked at her hand as it held the driving wheel, and the ring sparkled in the sunlight, her evidence of Mathew's love for her and of hers for him. Tears streamed from her face as the car continued to speed along. She only hoped that Rosemary's husband would accept her into his home after he heard her story because she knew that Rosemary wouldn't have trouble letting her stay over for a few months until her baby was born.

Whilst tears continued to pour from her face, she held her stomach and gently rubbed it, the baby which was inside was a symbol of her and Mathew's love. He had been so happy to learn of the baby and there was no way that she would give up on it. For Mathew, she resolved to go on farther the road, to face any obstacle ahead, and to have his baby. Because for the love they had shared, no matter how minimal the time, was indeed magical.

About the Author

Prince Henry Chilonga, is a Clinician, Programs Coordinator, Health Adviser and a published author of Success Within Oneself (Self-help Non-Fiction Novel). He lives with his family in Lusaka, Zambia. He is a Passionate Writer, Entrepreneur and Health practitioner.

Prince Henry Chilonga's other works are: Success Within Oneself (Self-help Non-Fiction Novel) and Miss Pretty (Romance Fiction Short-stories). He is currently writing Behind Med-Scenes (Medical Fantasy Fiction Novel).

You can find his works on Amazon, Smashwords, Banes&Noble and connect with him on his email: chilongaprincehenry@gmail.com or on his official Facebook page: Prince Henry Chilonga.

www.ingramcontent.com/pod-product-compliance
Lightning Source LLC
La Vergne TN
LVHW010605160826
845677LV00013B/3258

* 9 7 9 8 3 7 1 0 0 9 2 8 9 *